DEVIANT

DEVIANT

Helen FitzGerald

Published in the United States in 2013 by Soho Teen
an imprint of
Soho Press, Inc.
853 Broadway
New York, NY 10003

Library of Congress Cataloging-in-Publication Data

FitzGerald, Helen.
Deviant / Helen FitzGerald.
p. cm
ISBN 978-1-61695-139-9 (alk. paper)
eISBN 978-1-61695-140-5

1. Science fiction. 2. Families—Fiction. 3. Behavior—Fiction.
I. Title.
PZ7.F575De 2013
[Fic]—dc23 2012033455

Interior design by Janine Agro, Soho Press, Inc.

Printed in the United States of America

10 9 8 7 6 5 4 3 2 1

For Alessandro Gillies, Luisa Gillies, and Squidgy the pig

CHAPTER ONE

The guy facing Abigail across the desk wasn't her parent and he wasn't her friend. "Sit down, Abi," he said, in a voice that tried to be both. He wasn't a social worker either, more an unqualified asshole. He did the Saturday night shifts. He slept when he was supposed to be keeping an eye on the residents. Abigail could get him sacked. Maybe she would if he called her Abi again.

"Abigail," she corrected him, settling into the chair. She didn't approve of nicknames. Nicknames were for people who were loved.

"Okay, Abigail. There, are you comfortable?"

"I'm okay."

"I have very bad news, I'm afraid."

She didn't respond.

"Abi?"

"I told you, it's Abigail," she said. Very bad news bored her, the certainty and regularity of it. It always came in counsel rooms like this: vomit-resistant carpet, untidy desks marked with coffee cup rings, stained ceilings. The Samaritan's poster on the wall with the suicide hotline. Always delivered by people like this: faces etched with fake concern that did not disguise the shopping lists being written in their heads.

At the Granoch Assessment Centre two years ago, she'd stared at the same stack of orange files, piled high. "*This residential school has an excellent reputation,*" that particular unqualified asshole had lied, "*and it's so close to where you grew up.*" As if closeness to a home long gone were a plus.

The orange file was scrawled with *Abigail Thom* in thick black pen with a five-digit code beneath: *50837*. That was her number. She was that number. Child fifty-thousand-eight-hundred-and-thirty-seven. Her crappy paper life: written by people who jotted as they spoke, who refused to let her see what they had written, and then went home at night, stopping first for their shopping. One day, she would like to read what was inside. What gave them the right to know what she didn't?

"Your mother died last night," he said.

Abigail heard the words, but could only focus on the coffee mug. GLASGOW, CITY OF CULTURE 1990. The mug was older than she was.

"This is very difficult to take in, I know." He paused before repeating the news. "Did you hear me? Your mother died last night. Your birth mother."

"Oh." It came out wrong. Too soft. She swallowed, sat upright. She attempted to merge the whimper into something disarming and matter-of-fact. "Oh, okay. Well thank you for telling me. Is that all?"

Unqualified Asshole blinked. He had obviously been hoping

for a big scene. He'd probably assumed she'd throw herself at him and cry onto his thin, bony shoulders. He was probably looking forward to going home and telling his roommate (no way did he have a girlfriend) that he had consoled a sixteen-year-old orphan, that he had held her tight while she sobbed; that he, and only he, had *helped* today.

"Um, well actually, the nurse said your mother left something for you at the Western Infirmary. Do you want me to take you there to pick it up?"

"No," Abigail said. "I know where it is."

THE HOSPITAL WAS A five-minute walk from New Life Hostel, which she'd been forced to call home this last year. *No* Life Hostel, as she put it. Six bedrooms, twelve residents. While the residents were known as *Homeless Young Adults* or *Care Leavers* or *The Looked After*, Abigail preferred the truth to euphemisms: *Unloved Nobodies*.

She'd been an unloved nobody since nine, when Nieve died. Lovely Nieve. Until then, Abigail had hardly ever even thought of her birth mother. Nieve was a middle-aged hippie. A greying long-haired lady who smoked pot and played guitar. Kind, caring, and giving. All Abigail had ever known and all she ever needed. Yes, their life was "unconventional" (social worker's word); they lived on an anti-nuclear camp in Western Scotland. US submarines were still based in the area, even though the Soviet Union was dead and gone. No threat, so why were there ships of war? A protest community had taken root to try and get them out.

Nieve's bright pink caravan bore the slogan "NO NUKES!" in black paint. There were beds at the far end. Abigail had slept in the top bunk, with a wee window overlooking the Holy Loch. Nieve made Scotch broth that simmered on the gas cooker. Abigail picked mushrooms in the autumn with the other kids. They sat by bonfires at night, told stories, walked to school together. Adults did the same except for the school part, spending the daylight hours plotting to make the world a better and safer and more just place.

Odd that Abigail couldn't remember anything beyond the first names of her childhood mates. Serena. Malcolm. Sunday, the baby.

Who knew where they were now, what they'd become?

Not long after Abigail's ninth birthday, Nieve told Abigail she had cancer.

Within a month, she was dead.

ABIGAIL HURRIED FROM UNQUALIFIED Asshole's office. She had to figure out what to do. Should she go to the hospital now? It was close, only blocks away in the same posh, trendy part of Glasgow. Both the Western Infirmary and No Life occupied beautiful Victorian buildings that disguised the misery within.

Her mother had been so near when she'd died. But then, Abigail had no idea where her mother had been living or what she'd been doing. Ever. Sixteen years ago, she'd arrived at Nieve's protest camp on a rainy Tuesday. She and Nieve were friends. According to Nieve, her mother had begged her friend to take the newborn baby. Her mother had been desperate and secretive. "*Keep her safe. Don't tell her anything about me. And never try to contact me.*"

Was that even true? Abigail hadn't wondered until now. Nieve hadn't been above lying.

After Nieve's death, Abigail was visited by two men in jeans. They drove her away in a battered Ford Fiesta. They were social workers, they told her. They were taking her to a place called "Care." She had no idea what they meant, but even at the age of nine, she quickly learned it was bad. It was that office with its dirty coffee mugs, orange files, and Samaritan's posters. She hadn't even been allowed to attend Nieve's funeral, a Humanist service near Tighnabruaich.

The ceremony would be full of drugs, they said. It was in her "best interests" to stay away.

That night, or so she imagined, their little community celebrated Nieve's life by painting her cardboard coffin.

Abigail had few regrets. But missing out on that still filled her with rage. She'd planned to paint two birds, flying free in clear blue sky, a copy of the image engraved on Nieve's "chest of special things" at the foot of her bed. Nieve had always told her that the two of them were a pair of free birds like the one in the carving. But the social workers said she couldn't go back to the commune or have any more contact with it.

And so it began. Seven years of being "looked after" in eight different places. Seven years of being examined and documented by early shift workers, late shift workers, night shift workers, field workers, adoption and fostering workers and blah, blah, blah. Mumbo Jumbo: all of it and all of them. What was it that the Bible said? "Seven lean years?" Maybe the Bible wasn't a total load of shite.

Her first social worker—one of the men in the Ford Fiesta—was Jason McVeigh. Long-haired and laid-back, like the men she had known on the anti-nuclear commune. Abigail felt comfortable with him. He gave her compassion and time. He listened to her opinions. He stood up for her when care workers accused her of stealing money from the staff office. (She hadn't.) Jason took her shopping when she had nothing to wear to the sad little dance her school held.

After two years, Jason left to work at a bar in Majorca. Who could blame him? He seemed choked up when he said good-bye. He would never forget her, he said.

Three years later, Abigail bumped into him at Central Station in Glasgow. He'd cut his hair short. He was pushing a buggy with a baby in it. *His* baby. Abigail raced up to him, excited. He looked as though he was trying hard, but he could not remember her name. All he could offer was a vacant smile and a "*Hope you're doing well?*"

Abigail had never gotten close to anyone after that. She gave up asking to go to the commune. By the time she was fourteen and living in the Granoch Assessment Centre a few kilometers down the road, she'd all but stopped remembering.

Abigail sat on her stiff, institutional twin bed. She had the room to herself right now, a good thing. Roommates and rooms blended from one to the next. Nobody, nothing ever quite managed to be clean. Not clean in the way people or places looked on TV, or even on the commune, where Nieve and her friends bathed in the Loch and took care to scrub and sanitize their mobile homes.

Her newest roommate, a freshly arrived Romanian girl named Camelia, was glued to the television in the common area.

The photo, Abigail kept thinking.

"Your mum was a good woman," Nieve had told her more than once, "but she wasn't able to look after you. Please don't ask me anything else."

At first Abigail didn't need to ask more. Nieve was her family. She belonged to someone. But for some reason, on her ninth birthday, Abigail had decided she wanted to know what her mother looked like.

"Please! As a birthday present?"

"I'm sorry, darling, I can't tell you anything. I promised."

"Nieve. *Please.*"

Reluctantly, Nieve removed the key—always attached to the silver chain around her neck—and for the first time Abigail could remember, Nieve unlocked the "chest of special things." It was her pride and joy, this thing, its heavy lid engraved with those birds, wings outstretched. And yet its contents were a mystery. Abigail tried to peek over Nieve's shoulder. All she saw was a bunch of junk photos, papers, and trinkets.

Nieve reached inside and handed Abigail a small, framed Polaroid: colorful protesters in Glasgow's George Square with NO NUKES! placards.

"That's me at the very front, and that's her, there, the pretty one, third from the left in the second row. See? In orange and red? Same build as you?"

Abigail scrunched her eyes to look at the tiny red and orange protester.

"She has the same slender figure as you, see!" Nieve said. "Thank God for small favors."

Nine-year-old Abigail could only confirm that the woman in the photo was indeed slim and that her features were regular. As for pretty, she couldn't really tell. *This is my mother?* she remembered wondering.

Nieve was already dying then. And she knew it.

Abigail glanced at her grey Nike backpack at the foot of the bed. The photo was tucked in the side pocket. Apart from Nieve's silver chain with the key on it—which Abigail had worn around her neck since Nieve's death—it was the only memento she kept of anything remotely resembling "family." She unzipped the backpack. Her fingers did not tremble. They were remarkably steady. She touched the frame, turned it around and opened it, retrieving the small piece of paper she'd hidden there several years ago: a cut-out photocopy of her mother's face enlarged and enlarged again. Abigail had made the copy in the office of her fourth children's home while the care workers were dealing with a fight in the girls' bathroom.

It was a blur.

Her mother was a blur. An after-image.

Abigail grabbed her coat from the hall. Camelia was watching *Arachnophobia*. Abigail could relate; she'd spent many hours on the same couch watching the only DVD she owned:

The Shining. A family of three, snowbound in a cursed hotel for the winter, forced to cope with Jack Nicholson's terrifying descent into violent madness. Abigail had always loved it, though not because she felt trapped. She loved it for the wee boy, Danny. He had the "shining": a psychic ability to read the future, see into the past, and communicate telepathically with those who had it, too. It was this power that enthralled—to be so close to someone that she could see the whole of that person's mind, and that person hers. A nonsensical pipe dream. God, she wasn't even close enough to anyone to communicate properly with words.

Camelia fidgeted at the hairy spider legs on the screen.

She should be nervous. Dirt-poor with a mother in desperate need of medical help, Camelia had posted on the web that she was seeking a job to support her family back in Romania. Within hours, she had a "boyfriend": Billy, who fell in love with her sight unseen, compensated her for her ticket, picked her up at the airport, then dumped her at the hostel with an "I'll be back shortly." Camelia had been waiting on the sofa ever since.

Billy was very well-known at No Life. He was twenty-seven or so, with the stocky physique of a rugby player and the slang of a boy who'd stopped going to school not long after being toilet trained. No one ever called him a pimp, but he was. No one ever called him a human trafficker, but he was. Abigail had shared bedrooms with two of Billy's previous "girlfriends." One had died of an overdose. The other was still selling herself on Glasgow Green. Billy's strategy was to meet girls online or at the hostel, rootless and homeless and perfect little earners. He would get them hooked and send them off to the street.

He'd tried this routine with Abigail shortly after she'd arrived at No Life, offering a hit for free. She'd told him what he could do with himself.

Abigail stared at Camelia. The poor girl chewed a cracked fingernail, compulsively glancing out the window and checking the clock on her phone.

This isn't my problem.

OUTSIDE IT WAS RAINING: surprise, surprise. God, she hated this city.

"My mother is dead," Abigail said out loud as she walked along the leafy street, wondering if this might make her feel something, anything. It didn't.

"My mother is dead," Abigail said again. She sloshed past the Kelvingrove Art Gallery. Apparently the man who designed this beautiful red sandstone building had killed himself afterward. They'd made it the wrong way around, rumor had it. Nonsense, obviously, as both sides were identical. If he'd killed himself, it wasn't because of the building. It was because he wanted to. And at the end of the day, who wouldn't?

"So she's dead," Abigail said out loud. "So what? Who gives a shit?"

Glasgow dripped onto Abigail as she walked the three blocks to the hospital. The rain coated her with memories. When she was thirteen, she'd asked the residential workers if she could have a picnic in Queen's Park. Not only did it rain, but one of her nobody friends slashed another of her nobody friends with the birthday cake knife. The whole gathering ended up waiting in Accident and Emergency for four hours. Yet the social workers couldn't understand why she preferred to sit alone in her crap room and read.

In her second-to-last year at the residential school in Granoch, having learned quite a bit on her own, she asked if she could take chemistry *and* physics. But the timetables clashed. It was surprising they had the science subjects at all, considering some pupils her age were still reading *Spot the Dog*. In the Principal's office, she argued calmly at first, then not so calmly, and then called the Principal a bloody idiot. As a result, she was banned from taking either subject. That night, she waited till it was dark and jumped out the dormitory window. She ran as far away as her legs would take her. The police found her a day later, sitting among the shattered glass of a vandalized bus shelter, drenched from the rain, and starving.

Will I die here? she wondered. Soaked in a polluted drizzle? Would she be burnt in a crematorium overlooked by decaying high-rises? Would the wet clumps of her body ash be tossed to concrete?

The better question was: Why wouldn't she?

Glasgow University bore down with its wise and unseen eyes. She had never been inside, but often she'd watched from the sidewalk as students strolled along stone-pillared open-air corridors. Straight-shouldered and purposeful, *they* were clean. Taken care of. They were part of the sandstone columns, manicured walkways, and antique wooden doors. Now she could see their silhouettes in the cozy bar windows; now the grand spire of the university loomed over her from Gilmorehill, as if declaring: "*You will never come to me. You are just another aban-doned Glaswegian. You are a care-leaver, a homeless teenager, and now, an orphan. You think you're clever? Well you're not. You will never read inside me.*"

Well, screw the university. Their loss. Screw the whole lot. Who's to say there wasn't some posh version of Billy getting rich girls hooked on smack in there?

She turned away, dodging puddles. She wondered if her mother's body would still be at the hospital. She wondered if she would have to look at it.

"My name is Abigail Thom. My mother, Sophie Thom, died here last night. Apparently she left something for me."

The receptionist tapped away at the computer before direct-ing her up the stairs to the second floor and then to the nurses' station in Ward B. There, Abigail repeated the above sentence, word for word.

"Can you spell that?" asked the pinched-faced nurse.

"Of course I can."

The nurse didn't find this funny. She was Scottish, after all. Scots didn't find funny things funny. Scots liked to be miser-able. Why else did they play the bagpipes? Why else did they drink and smoke themselves into early graves? Why else did they pledge undying love to crap soccer teams that failed at everything but religious bigotry?

"A-B-I-G . . ."

"Not you, your mother."

"Oh. D-E-A-D."

The nurse had typed three of the four letters into her computer before raising her eyebrows and looking up from above her cheap glasses. "I'm very busy."

"It's Sophie. S-O-P-H-I-E."

"Last name?"

"Thom. T-H-O-M."

"Just a moment." The nurse tapped into the computer.

Abigail looked around her. Ten beds lined each side of the room, curtains in between, some drawn, some not. The beds were all occupied. All the women looked the same: withered, yellow, and 173 years old. Her mother had probably been in one of those beds. Which one?

"Follow me."

The smell of antiseptic was even stronger in the private room than in the ward. Perhaps they doused the rooms of the dead with an extra bottle. There was a window at one end overlooking the murky River Clyde and its ominous ship-building cranes. There, below it, was a single bed under a buzzing fluorescent light and a sheet-covered body.

As if in a dream, Abigail walked to the head of the bed, lifted the sheet, and looked down at the face. She felt a flicker of the faintest recognition from the photo. But this woman was old, a stranger. Her eyes were closed. Her lashes were thick and black, no mascara. Her eyebrows were full, nice shape. Abigail stared. Her mother had plucked a little, yes, but not much. No need.

Hmm, so that's where my tiny pinned-back ears come from.

Had she tattooed lip liner onto her lips? They were full, and defined at the edges. Not thin Scottish lips at all. Exactly like Abigail's, in fact. She could see from the shape of the sheet that her mother's once-slim build was now emaciated, dead-thin.

She'd imagined meeting her mother many times. Never like this. Was she beautiful? Can a dead face be beautiful? Her hair was still a lovely, raven black. But mostly, she was dead, and, no, dead cannot be beautiful.

After gazing at the face for another ten seconds or so, Abigail turned and walked toward the door.

"Wait!" the nurse called, replacing the sheet. "She left you something, remember?"

Abigail stopped but didn't turn around. The nurse retrieved a plastic bag from the bedside cabinet and handed it to her.

"Thank you," Abigail choked out. And then she was hurtling through the corridor and down the stairs so fast that she had to lean against the brick wall of the hospital when she finally made it outside. Her breath came in heavy gasps. She realized she was clutching an old, thinning Tesco supermarket bag. There was something square and heavy inside.

Calming herself, she walked down the hill and across the road into the park. The rain had stopped, but she didn't notice. Climbing over a fence into the woodland by the river, she found a spot under a tree and emptied the Tesco bag of its contents: a thick padded package about twenty centimeters square. Abigail laid the plastic bag on the wet grass, sat down on it, and examined the package. It was inscribed with a thick, black marker.

For my daughter Abigail Thom: URGENT!!!

She picked at the sticky brown tape and tore it off.

Money. *Jesus.* Abigail's eyes widened. Her heart fluttered. British Pounds, lots of them, bundle after bundle after bundle of twenties.

One of the bundles fell to the ground. She glanced around the shadowy park, afraid that someone may have seen her— then scooped it up with trembling fingers and shoved it all back in the supermarket bag. She scrambled closer to the river and knelt in the mud, no longer worried about getting wet or dirty. The park was deserted. She unfolded the typed letter that had come with the package. Inside the letter was an American Airlines e-ticket. She gripped it as she read.

Dear Abigail,

I don't know where to start, so I won't tell you the beginning. I'll just tell you the end. There are five things I want you to know:

Your father is alive. His name is Grahame Johnstone. He lives in Los Angeles. I was going to wait until you turned eighteen to tell you about him but I will be dead. Very soon, I think. I only told your father about you yesterday, the 18th July. For everyone's sakes, you need to know him.

You have an older sister called Becky. Please show her this letter. Please tell her I love her, as I love you, that I still remember her beautiful face, and that I have thought about you both every day. She was an inquisitive and determined baby. Ask for her help.

The ticket in this envelope is a one-way ticket to Los

Angeles. Your father is expecting you. He will collect you from the airport. He is a clever man, Abigail.

I saved £25,000 each, for you and Becky. Please don't tell your father about the money. It is your and your sister's inheritance, from me. Please accept your father's kindness. He will be kind to you. Use this money to be happy, use it to be free.

No matter what you and Becky think of me now, I know with all my heart that you will feel differently one day. I do love you, Abigail. I have always loved you.

Her mother signed a squiggle at the bottom of the letter. A signature, in black pen. *No wonder she typed the letter,* Abigail thought. Her handwriting! It was terrible, almost illegible, with little flecks of ink everywhere. She must have been very sick. With all the shaky markings, it almost looked more like *Stophie Them* than *Sophie Thom.*

CHAPTER TWO

For a very long while, Abigail sat alone by the river. She read the letter once, twice—over and over. Each time she had a different reaction.

Her mother had loved her.

Her mother was a junkie, or a drunk.

Her mother made no sense.

Her mother was dead.

Her mother was crazy.

Her mother was a liar.

Her mother had obviously NEVER loved her.

The e-ticket was American Airlines flight number 3846, leaving Glasgow Airport at 10 P.M.

Tomorrow.

Abigail looked at her watch. Nine thirty P.M. She grabbed the bag of money with her free hand, gently clutching the ticket and the letter to her chest. She scurried up the riverbank, through the woods, jumped the fence, and ran all the way back to the hostel.

The care-worker was talking to a friend on the phone. "Oh hi, Abi," he said, returning to his conversation. His concern over her bereavement had obviously run its course, or else he'd forgotten. She didn't have time to argue with him about her name. She ran into her room, slammed the door shut, and sat on the bed to get her head together. Could she trust her mother? This letter? Did she really have a father and a sister in Los Angeles? She glanced around. The window was painted shut and so filthy she could hardly see through it. There were no pictures or posters on the walls, only the marks where previous residents had placed theirs. Camelia's narrow bed was unmade, the cheap nylon sheets stained from years of God-knows-what. Staff didn't bother nagging residents to launder their sheets or make their beds. But Abigail didn't need to be nagged; she washed her linen once a week and made her bed first thing every morning.

Routine was all she had. This grotty hellhole was all she had.

Right. Even if the letter was total shite, she had to get out. A crap situation in America was better than a crap situation here. And, the money was real.

What would she need? Her thick jacket? No, not for LA. Her books? Since arriving at No Life, she'd borrowed three books every week from the local library to keep her brain from rotting: two serious, one lighthearted. This week they were *The Principles of Biochemistry, The Silence of the Lambs,* and *Funny Physics Problems.* She stuffed them inside her backpack. (She loathed stealing on principle, but the library could replace them; besides, the staff always gave her dirty looks whenever she hung around the stacks too long.) What else? *The Shining*

DVD, of course. Her black Fly boots? They were full-on winter wear. But she loved them! She'd wear them on the flight,
even though it was midsummer. She'd wear her dark grey com-
bats, her STUFF THE MONARCHY T-shirt, and her cropped black
leather jacket. Her favorite outfit.

She threw some underwear, spare T-shirts, and socks in the
back, then tucked the money, letter, and e-ticket into the side
pocket beside Nieve's photo. She checked the chest of drawers
and the tiny sagging rail in the wardrobe she shared with Camelia. Nothing important there. No personal effects. Nothing
sentimental. What was the point in gathering things when
she knew she wouldn't be staying anywhere for any length of
time? Abigail's essentials, her whole world, couldn't even fill
a backpack. Last, she went to the bathroom and added her
toothbrush, toothpaste, and Fibre Putty hair product.

Stick to the routine. Invent a new one. Abigail could see
herself as if looking into a mirror. She snapped into a kind of
robot mode under stress. She became methodical, neat, dili-
gent. Most people found it creepy, which also suited her just
fine. They left her alone.

Now, she made a mental list to make sure everything was
in order. She retrieved the e-ticket from the backpack pocket.

Ten P.M. tomorrow. Yep, plenty of time.

The length of the flight would be eleven hours. The books
would keep her busy.

Was her luggage the right size and weight? No way could
this flimsy backpack weigh more than thirty-five pounds, even
with the books.

But when her eyes reached the bottom of the e-ticket, her heart froze: VALID PASSPORT REQUIRED.

Why had her mother not thought about this? Why on earth *would* Abigail have a passport? As if kids who are abandoned by their mothers get to go on skiing holidays in Switzerland and summer camps in France! As if she'd ever had the opportunity to get out of this godforsaken country! Sunnier, wealthier, happier Edinburgh was only fifty miles away, and she'd never even made it *there*. (Once, the care workers at Netherall House organized a trip to Loch Lomond. Abigail was excited. It turned out to be a twenty-minute drive. In a minivan. Normal schoolchildren in full-sized buses laughed at them en route. The minivan full of "special" children eventually parked in a deserted lot. The ten children got out and threw stones into the lake. It rained. They drove home.)

She had been nowhere, done nothing. She'd be *stuck* nowhere if she didn't find a passport. *Shite*. She couldn't snap out of robot mode. Now she had to focus.

Abigail poked her head in the hall. Camelia was in the television room. Several other girls were sprawled on the frayed, red-fabric sofas, watching a twenty-year-old soft-core porn show called *Eurotrash*. The teenagers watched the ten-ton television set all day here—hungover from drinking and drug-taking, comatose with bloodshot eyes. Staff never questioned it. It kept them quiet. Camelia had put makeup and a coat on since Abigail had last seen her, and was standing at the window.

"Camelia, can you come here?" Abigail called.

Her roommate flinched and blinked, then quickly rushed over

to the door. Unlike the other residents, her eyes were alert. She was new, thank God: a junk and misery virgin. She still had hope.

"Have you heard from Billy?" Abigail asked.

"Billy is coming here to get me." Camelia's English was stilted but understandable.

"When did he say that?"

Camelia looked at the clock on her phone. "Five hours ago."

"Do you know where he is?"

"His text say he caught up in a meeting in town?" she answered, as if posing another question. Her accent thickened with her uncertainty.

"A meeting, right. He'll be at the Solid Bar."

Camelia's eyes brightened. "You take me to the Solid Bar? You know where it is?"

Abigail said simply, "No, I'm not going to take you to see him. Billy does not love you. He is not your boyfriend."

She blinked again and tried to smile. "What do you mean?"

"Exactly what I said," Abigail stated.

"I don't understand you. Billy and I, we are together, you understand? He pays for my ticket here—"

"Come with me," Abigail interrupted. "Come and talk."

Closing the door behind them, Abigail sat Camelia down on her bed. She tried to offer a smile, but her heart was pounding. "Listen. I don't have much time. But I want you to know: when I look at you, I see girls who have died. Please listen to me, Camelia. You're not the first girl Billy has done this to. He targets girls who have nothing to lose. The girls who end up here. He gets them hooked on heroin. You know what heroin is? Smack? And then he gets them to sell their bodies."

Camelia's heavily made-up face darkened. "I know what heroin is. But you are not right. Billy helps me get a job and brings my family over here. My mother is very sick."

Abigail shook her head as patiently as she could. "He's not. He's a bad, bad guy."

"No," Camelia snapped. "I heard the other girls say you're strange. Leave me alone." She stood and reached for the door.

Abigail chewed her lip. "Okay," she blurted out. "You want to see him? Fine, I'll take you there."

THE BUS SHELTER HAD no glass and no roof, and the rain had started up again. Camelia's mood soured significantly by the time she and Abigail reached the Solid Bar an hour later, soaked to the skin. The warm wind had turned the rain horizontal, obscuring the view of the tenement flats on Argyll Street and the long, dreary queue of shops on Sauchiehall Street.

As suspected, Billy was sitting with a young girl at the back of the dark, narrow pub. Rock music blared from television screens in the dark corners. The place stank of booze. Billy rubbed the girl's arm, looking completely wasted. If he'd been brought up somewhere different, maybe he would have been handsome. The basics were there, certainly: dark hair, deep brown eyes. Abigail imagined his Facebook profile pic might seem quite appealing. But he'd grown up in Glasgow. It had muddied him, made him ugly.

Camelia stiffened a little.

"Don't get upset," Abigail whispered as she pulled her toward him. "What you're learning now might save your life."

Billy's glassy eyes zeroed in on Abigail. "Well, look who it is, Mother Theresa!" His pet nickname for her ever since she refused to inject. He blinked and tried to straighten, noticing Camelia. He stopped rubbing his companion. "Hello! What are you doing here?"

"She's been waiting for you," Abigail snapped. "You were supposed to collect her, remember? You were supposed to help her because you love her?"

"Sorry I got waylaid, sweetheart," Billy slurred, his blood-shot gaze still on Camelia.

"I told her everything about you, Billy," Abigail continued evenly. "What you do with your girlfriends. She doesn't believe me."

He sneered. "What you on about?"

Abigail turned her attention to the girl sitting beside Billy. The bags under her eyes matched her thick, badly applied eye-liner. Another three weeks, maybe two, and Camelia would be in the exact same place. But this girl was even younger than they were. Fifteen, maybe.

"Get out of here," Abigail snapped.

The girl rolled her eyes dramatically. Then she took some money from her bra and handed it to Billy, planting a sloppy kiss on his cheek. With that, she raised a finger at Abigail and Camelia. They watched as she staggered out in the rain.

Billy just laughed. "Now get out, Mother Theresa. I want

some time with ma bird." He ushered Camelia to sit beside him. "C'mere, Amelia."

"Camelia," the girl corrected, her voice shaking. "You *bou . . . carule . . . Bagate-as in mormant.*"

Abigail placed herself in between them in case Camelia was tempted to smash Billy in the face. "He's not worth it. Go and wait for me at the door. I won't be long,"

Eyes blazing, Camelia stomped out. Once the door swung shut behind her, Abigail turned back. "I need a passport. It's urgent. I have to have it by two P.M. tomorrow."

"Wit!" Billy laughed as he exhaled smoke. He peered over her shoulder, trying to spot the girl who'd trotted off into the rain. "It takes days to get those sorted. And it's expensive. Talking money, you owe me for that girl. Her ticket cost nearly two hundred quid."

"If you get me the passport, I'll give you a thousand."

"Hmm." Billy took a long drag and said, "Uh-uh, cannae do it for that. No way."

Abigail turned and reached into her bag, shakily counting out £2,000 with only her back as protection. "This is all I have," she lied, making sure to keep the other wads of cash hidden from him. "Two K, if you get it to me by two P.M. tomorrow. I'll meet you here. And if you disappoint me, I swear I'll come back here every night and day, scaring your girlfriends away until you're broke or dead—whichever comes first."

He stubbed out his cigarette and looked at the cash. He smiled at Abigail, then at Camelia's back in the rain-soaked window. Finally he nodded and extended a hand to shake.

She did not reciprocate. Instead, she divided the money into two piles, pushed one toward him, and said, "Half now, half tomorrow. Here. Two o'clock."

Before he could protest, she strode from the bar and took Camelia's arm, hurrying back to the bus stop. It was no bluff, her threat. She only hoped it was enough to scare Billy into coming through. But it probably was. He knew she made good on her promises.

THE HOSTEL WAS EMPTY when they returned, except for a night shift worker Abigail had never met before. Coincidentally he happened to be flipping through her orange file. He put it down nervously, embarrassed to be caught.

"Hello." He extended a hand. This one, she did shake. "I'm Arthur." He was new to the world of social work, obviously. He wanted to talk to them, get all their gory details. "You want a cup of tea, girls?"

Abigail recognized the look of morbid fascination on his middle-class face. Beneath it was a dollop of fear.

"No thanks, Arthur. Bath and bed."

She took Camelia's hand and escorted her to the downstairs bathroom. "By the way, what did you call Billy back there?"

"A *bou*—a castrated bull. I told him he's an ass and I want to put him in an early grave. I want to do this so much. You cannot understand how much I want to do this."

Abigail squeezed Camelia's fingers and let go. "He'll do it himself, honey. Two years tops. Save yourself the bother."

Camelia swallowed, blinking back tears and shaking her head.

"It's a big day tomorrow. We're going to get a good night's sleep," Abigail went on. She set about scrubbing the iron bath of its brown stains and clearing hair clumps and soap bits before running the water. "Have a good soak. I'll use the one upstairs."

"Big day for you, yes," Camelia said. "But what am I going to do?"

"You're going to go home."

"But I can't. I have no money . . ." Camelia began to tremble. She wiped her cheek.

The bath was full. Abigail turned off the taps. "Don't cry. Get in. I've got money. I can get you home. You dodged a bullet, missus. You're gonna get out of this place. Everything's going to be fine."

ABIGAIL COULDN'T SLEEP. SHE eventually gave up trying. She lay still in the darkness, Camelia snoring softly across the room. Her thoughts raced. Her mother was dead; she was leaving her country; she had a father, a sister . . . If she ever fell asleep and woke again, would it all be a dream? Or part of the same old nightmare?

Better not to think. Better to create a new routine that fit the situation.

She made lists in her head. She'd arranged to get the passport at 2 P.M., but didn't really need it until later. Billy wasn't known for his punctuality. So tomorrow, she'd have several hours to do the things she now realized she needed to do.

———

As soon as the sun rose, Abigail woke Camelia. After breakfast, she escorted her to the travel agency, where Abigail purchased a one-way ticket to Romania. Both Camelia and the travel agent gaped at the cash. At least the travel agent didn't ask questions. Neither did Camelia. After that, Abigail dragged Camelia with her to the hospital, explaining about her mother's death, the bizarre inheritance, and the ticket to America along the way.

Camelia didn't ask questions then, either. Maybe she didn't understand. Not surprising; Abigail hardly understood, herself.

The sterile hospital chamber smelled the same, looked the same, but the bed was bare and empty. Abigail stood staring at the place where her dead mother had lain. Nothing but crisp clean sheets. She might as well have never been there at all.

A nurse came in. "Excuse me, it's not visiting hours. Can I help you?"

"A woman called Sophie Thom died in this room. I forgot to ask about the ashes. Is she being cremated?"

"Sophie. Yes. In fact . . ." The nurse looked at her watch. "Her funeral is happening now, at Lambhill Crematorium. If you hurry . . ."

"Right, thanks." On her way out, Abigail turned and asked, "By the way, what did she die of exactly?"

"I'm sorry, but I'm not authorized."

Abigail almost laughed. "I'm her daughter."

"You're Abigail?"

"Yes."

"She told me about you and Becky."

Abigail's breath caught in her throat. "Becky? What did she tell you?"

"Strange things. She was delirious toward the end."

"Tell me what she said." Abigail only now realized that she was still blocking Camelia's exit with her arm.

"She kept saying, '*It's all up to the girls now.*'"

"So was she crazy?" Abigail pressed. "Tell me, please, how did she die?"

"It was cancer. Your mother had breast cancer. She was very brave."

Cancer? Abigail tried to process the word. A normal way to die. Shitty, but normal. And subject to all sorts of factors and change. So what was with the urgency? What was with the suspicious cash and the exact timetable mentioned in the letter?

"You'd better hurry," the nurse said, checking her watch again.

THE TAXI DRIVER WAS pleased with the tip. Funny how money made everything so easy. Abigail had paid him double to step on it. He called a cheery thanks as the two girls jumped out of the car and ran inside the crematorium.

Hearing music, Abigail opened the door on the left of the foyer. The room was packed with wailing grievers. A family member was reading a eulogy. At the foot of the coffin stood a flower-drenched easel with a picture of a smiling teenage boy. Wrong room. She ran out again and pushed the other door.

Camelia still hadn't uttered so much as a peep since Abigail had dragged her from No Life. Part of her was relieved and not all that surprised. Another part wanted to know what this very sad Romanian immigrant thought of all this madness.

There were no grievers in here. Just a minister and a coffin that was slowly disappearing through a purple velvet curtain toward an abyss of flickering flames. Another man stood at the back behind a pillar. All she could see was some blond hair. It almost looked as if he were hiding. Maybe he was lost. Abigail sat in the front row. Camelia slid in beside her.

"Should I say goodbye?" Abigail only realized she was speaking out loud when her voice caught. This was all happening too fast, too fast . . .

The coffin disappeared into the furnace.

The minister picked up his bible and walked out without as much as a sideways glance. There were no flowers, no pictures. She swallowed. *Funerals are supposed to be depressing, but this one takes the biscuit.* Abigail turned to the blond man. He was already halfway out the back door. She chased after him, Camelia on her heels. By the time they got outside, he'd jumped in a taxi. The back of his blond head disappeared down the long driveway.

Camelia must have seen the disappointment and sadness on her face. She reached for Abigail's arm.

Screw this.

Abigail marched back into the crematorium and asked the woman at reception if she could make arrangements to have her mother's ashes sent to her new address. She didn't know her new address yet. Nor did she know what she'd do with the ashes. But it had occurred to her the previous night that she should probably find a way to get them in case her newly discovered sister was as baffled by all this as she was.

The receptionist tapped on the computer. "I'm sorry. The next of kin has already requested the urn."

"Next of kin? Who?"

"I'm afraid I can't give you that information."

"She was my mother!" Abigail almost yelled. "How can you not give me that information?"

"If she was your mother," the receptionist said through clenched teeth that were asking to be knocked out, "then how could you not already know?"

Abigail's jaw dropped. Fortunately, Camelia dragged Abigail away from the desk and out the door before she could say a word.

"Come on," Camelia murmured. "We go. Leave it. It's nearly two o'clock."

THE TAXI REACHED THE Solid Bar at ten past two. Abigail's nerves had once again frozen into their standard unfeeling position. "Wait for me here and leave the meter running," she instructed.

Billy was drinking a pint in the same seat as yesterday. He wore the same Glasgow underworld uniform, labels displayed for the world to see (Jeans: Diesel; T-shirt: Calvin Klein; Overall Message to the Universe: Unoriginal). It was obvious that he hadn't washed. He probably hadn't slept since she'd last seen him either. His sockets were so dark and so deep that his eyes almost disappeared into his head. His greasy hair stuck up at the back. His cheek scar was red, irritated. Without a word, he slid a passport out of his pocket and slammed it on the table, trying to smile as if pleased. But he was jittery, haggard. Crank, probably.

Abigail reached for it.

"Uh-uh. Other half first," Billy snapped.

"Once I've looked at it," Abigail said, snatching it from his grasp and opening it.

For a split-second, she was almost tempted to laugh. She found herself squinting at a thirty-two-year-old red-haired woman called Alina Beklea. "What? Who? That's not me."

"Course it's not, ya numpty. Ya think I could get one with you in one day? Anyway, you didn't give me a photograph."

"You didn't ask for one."

"I'm supposed to think of everything?"

"But . . . I look *nothing* like this."

"I dunno, dye your hair, put thick makeup on, and way-hay Alina!"

"I have a ticket to LA in my name. Abigail Thom. This says Alina Beklea."

"Change your flight." He stubbed out his smoke and scowled. "Gimme time to get your photo and sort a passport with you on it."

Abigail glared at him. "My father is meeting me there."

"You got any more money?"

She didn't answer.

"Then, little miss goody-goody, *maybe* you should buy another plane ticket in the name of Alina Beklea."

Abigail sighed and counted out £300. "Good idea. That's what I'll do, which means the second half of your fee has just been significantly reduced." She tossed the money down at the bar, then turned and ran.

"Oy! Get back here," Billy yelled. "That's not right. I know where you're going, Mother Theresa. I know where you're ending up!"

Abigail lurched to a stop at the taxi window and tapped the glass. "Just gotta get something from the chemist," she gasped to Camelia. "I'll be two secs." She raced over to Central Station. The glass-roofed hall of the station was buzzing with pigeons and chatter. Hundreds of people stood in front of the timetable board, staring at it like robots as they waited for their platform number to appear. People like her. People running away from something; toward something; escaping something, everything. The chemist had about a thousand different types of hair dye. Abigail chose one that matched the color in the photograph, sprinted across the road, and jumped back in the taxi.

She had less than seven hours to make her flight.

ARTHUR, THE NEW GUY, was back on duty when they arrived.

"Hi, girls. We're making pancakes. Do you want to help?"

"No, thanks." Abigail spoke calmly, but her palms were clammy. "I'm dying my hair red. Think it'll suit me?"

"I think it will," he said with a smile.

She mustered a smile in return. Poor Arthur. He was helping in the kitchen. He was polite. He was motivated. No doubt all of that positivity would be sucked out within a year.

Camelia lay on her bed while Abigail waited for the dye to take hold. She had everything she needed now, except a ticket in the right name. She'd have to get to the airport early enough to purchase a new ticket. What time was it? Four P.M. already.

Suddenly, it dawned on Abigail that she was missing one vital item. Raising a finger to her lips, she tiptoed out of the room and scurried into the office. Five orange files were strewn across the desk. Flicking through them with one eye on the door (everyone was still making pancakes), she found hers, grabbed it, and ran back to her bedroom.

"What's that?" Camelia asked.

"Nothing." Abigail wrapped the orange file in a plastic bag and put it into her backpack. Still, she had to smile. *Now* she had everything she needed.

The alarm on Camelia's mobile phone went off. Her color was ready.

"Here, let me do your makeup." Camelia opened her Russian-made cosmetics bag. "You have such pretty face." She dabbed tiny dots of foundation and smoothed them with her soft fingers.

Abigail glanced at her reflection in Camelia's compact mirror. While her hair was the same color as Alina Beklea's, she did *not* look thirty-two years old.

"You have same mark as me," Camelia remarked, noticing the faint red discoloration on Abigail's arm.

"It was the last tetanus booster," Abigail said absently.

"I have same. I have all kinds of . . . how do you say?"

"Vaccines?"

Camelia nodded.

"Yeah. Health Services gives them to all of us—" Abigail broke off, about to say *Unloved Nobodies*. "Kids," she finished. "Chicken Pox. And the triple whammy." They rattled off the next three words in unison: "Measles, Mumps, Rubella." Abigail laughed. "So, Romania must not be all that different from Scotland." She pictured a rainy, downtrodden city. She pictured infant Camelia, sobbing as she was administered shots by a stranger. She pictured present-day Camelia, wandering back to a foster home alone, dripping wet, after her tetanus booster.

"Every place is the same," Camelia murmured. "But in my world, girls with lips like yours wear gloss!" Concentrating hard, she applied thick goo to Abigail's lips. No one had ever done this for her before. She had to admit, it felt wonderful. "Go mwah! Like this."

Abigail held up the mirror again and made the kissing noise requested.

Camelia laughed again. "Are you loving yourself?"

Abigail had to laugh, too. Not the phrase she would have used. But on the plus side, she no longer looked like Abigail Thom, orphan of the No Life Hostel. It was a start.

"Now, we have to make you ugly and old." Camelia was gentle as she worked her magic: using mascara, eyeliner, too much (green!) eye shadow, bright pink lipstick, three more coats of foundation, and blush.

"Now look!"

Blimey. Abigail checked herself one last time. She was old and ugly . . . just like the woman in the photo. She resisted the urge to jump up and hug her roommate.

It was nearly 6 P.M. Time to get going.

The hall was empty and all the doors were closed, so no one would see her go.

Thank God for small favors.

That was one of Nieve's favorite phrases. Abigail paused at the whiteboard in the hall. It was littered with photocopied pages of house rules, health and safety information, helpline numbers, leaflets about leaving care, employment agencies, immunizations, and drug counseling. She found the only clear spot, two inches by two inches, and wrote in tiny writing with the black marker: *I've gone to America. Keep safe. Abigail. x*

"Ready?" she said to Camelia.

Luggage in hand, they hurried through the empty hall and out the door. A taxi was waiting just outside. It was the first bit of good luck they'd had. Thank God for small favors, indeed.

"I WANT YOU TO take this." Abigail counted out £20,000 of the money her mother had left her in the backseat. After all, she still had another £25,000 for her sister, if she even existed.

Camelia didn't respond. She blinked at the pile of cash several times, then turned her head back to the window. "No. I can't."

"Take it," Abigail insisted.

"Why?"

"I don't want it. Save your mum's life. And your own. Use it to be happy and free, whatever that means."

Camelia shook her head. Abigail didn't prod. Finally, Camelia tore her gaze back to the worn leather upholstery and ran her finger along the top bundle of money. Looking up at Abigail, she smiled. "Thank you," she choked out. She reached to place her hand on Abigail's hand. "Thank you so—"

Abigail withdrew on instinct. She couldn't hug this girl. There was no point. Swallowing, she turned and opened her own window. She stuck her head out as the taxi made its way along the overpass that cut the grey city in half. She felt the Scottish wind on her face—for the last time, she hoped. She sighed at the River Clyde and the new monstrosities that had been built alongside it, designed to rejuvenate, but just adding to the city's blemishes. Glasgow was just like Billy. Unhealthy, angry, unhappy, scarred with wounds from lip to ear.

She breathed in the stale air as they hurtled along the motorway, passing nothing notable along the way, lots and lots and lots more of non-notable nothing.

"Good riddance, Glasgow!" Abigail yelled from her taxi window. "Good riddance, shithole of the world! Good fucking riddance!"

CHAPTER THREE

Abigail had never been inside an airport before. It felt like a hospital, but for happy, healthy people. A holding zone somewhere in between the real world and nothingness. And everyone except her was completely unimpressed with it, Camelia included. They'd all done it before, too, it seemed. Businessmen tapped at their cell phones; parents hustled toddlers away from chocolate displays; nobody looked where they were going. It was a big institution with rules she knew nothing about. She shifted on her feet as Camelia checked in for her 9 P.M. flight, feeling not unlike she did that first day in the care room at Dunoon.

"This is my mobile number and my email address," Camelia whispered once she had her boarding pass. She scribbled on a baggage address card, its little white string dancing as she wrote. "And this is my address in Romania. Please keep in touch. If there's ever anything I can do for you . . . anything, ever—"

"I will," Abigail interrupted. She shoved the piece of cardboard in her back pocket. "Now, get out of here!"

Camelia smiled at her. She leaned forward, as if to hug. Abigail said good-bye the only way she knew how. She turned and ran off.

THE QUEUE AT THE American Airlines counter was long and slow. Eight thirty P.M. by the time she was served. Only ninety minutes till takeoff. Luckily there were seats left on her flight, but only in first class, which meant Abigail had to fork out £2,111 for a one-way ticket to LA in the name of Alina Beklea. The woman at the desk was so flustered she hardly even looked at the phony passport. She shoved it into the scanner. There were no problems. *The power of cash*, Abigail thought to herself, feeling queasy. No questions asked, happy cab drivers, compliant sex traffickers. Amazing what you can get away with if you're hideously ugly and have enough money to buy a first-class ticket to America.

As Abigail moved away from the desk, her head began to spin. The crowd, the bright lights, the cavernous echo . . . *It's all too fast*, she thought again. She couldn't snap into robot mode. Forty-eight hours ago she'd been Abigail Thom, Unloved Nobody. Now she was Abigail Thom, heiress of a small cash fortune, with a father and sister waiting in America. She had to fight to breathe. *Los Angeles.* Was she really going there? To live? Was she really heading toward the international departure gate? Side-by-side with suits destined for hotels and affairs, with spoiled kiddies destined for theme parks?

Abigail's view of Los Angeles was based on the comedy channel. *Two and a Half Men* and *Entourage*, mainly. She imagined large beachside houses full of happily dysfunctional families. She imagined blue skies, oversized breakfasts, enthusiastic shop assistants, gorgeous posses of loyal friends eating salads while laughing loudly. Maybe she'd be doing that tomorrow. Laughing loudly in the sun over salad. Or maybe she'd simply wake up.

Just get on the plane.

Unfortunately, there was another, scarier queue to tackle. This involved a full-body scanning machine, like the kind they had in some young offender's facilities she'd seen. Officials with gadgets padded people down if they beeped. Uniformed men stared at a computer screen as bags moved along a conveyor belt. Abigail realized she was trembling. Once, she'd been searched in a police cell on suspicion of shoplifting in a supermarket. (She hadn't done it.) She hadn't just felt terrified, she'd felt violated. She could feel suspicious eyes boring down on her as she placed her backpack on the belt.

Just as she'd feared, a piercing beep erupted as she walked through the scanner.

A woman ushered her to stand on a black mat, where she waved a gadget over her body and frisked either side of her torso and legs.

"It's just your belt," the woman said. "You should take it off before you come through next time."

Abigail could only manage a nod.

The man at the scanning machine was unzipping her backpack and searching through it. Shit. Maybe Billy had sabotaged her, stuffed some drugs in while she wasn't looking.

"You have liquids in your bag." He held out the hair putty and toothpaste accusingly.

"Oh, is that bad?"

"Yes. It is. No liquids over 100 milliliters. This'll have to go." Before she could respond, he had tossed her Fibre Putty in the huge bin behind him. She couldn't help but notice that the bin was bursting with shampoo, conditioner, and skin lotion. There was even a bottle of wine. *They must divvy it out at the end of the day*, she thought to herself. A perk of the job.

"You can keep the toothpaste, but next time put it in the airport-issued plastic bag. Right?"

"Right. Ta." God, if there was ever a next time, there was a lot to remember. She shoved the toothpaste in her bag and zipped it up again.

Gate 43 was a ten-minute walk through brightly lit shops and featureless corridors with moving walkways. She took her seat in what looked like a doctor's waiting room. Peering out the huge windows into the night, she noticed the American Airlines plane attached to the gate. It was enormous. So high off the ground. She found herself scanning the body of the plane for faults. How would she even recognize a fault? She'd only watched one episode of *Air Crash Investigation*, and that particular plane had crashed due to weird insects nesting in some vital equipment.

"Flight 3845 to Los Angeles has been delayed," the air hostess at the gate desk announced over a loud speaker, "and will now depart at ten fifty-five P.M."

There was a collective sigh.

Bugger. Even longer to wait. As Abigail squirmed, she felt like a drug smuggler. A wrong move or a drop of sweat would bring in the sniffer dogs and police; any minute someone would discover she was not Alina Beklea and escort her back to No Life Hostel.

She tried to read her *Funny Physics* book, but couldn't concentrate. She tried to snooze; too nervous. Eventually, she looked at the clock and noticed there were only thirty-nine more minutes till takeoff. They'd have to board the plane any second now.

Two men in suits approached Gate 43 and seemed to be looking at her. Or maybe they weren't. She couldn't look back. She needed to do something to look normal.

An Internet point was located twenty feet along the corridor. She walked toward it as calmly as she could without looking at the men in suits. It cost a pound a minute, but Abigail used each second wisely.

In the Google search engine, she typed: "Grahame Johnstone."

Scrolling past a Grahame Johnstone on UK LinkedIn, a teenager on Bebo, a managing director of a Scottish roofing company, and a plumber from Cornwall, Abigail quickly adjusted her search to include "Los Angeles."

Hmm, perhaps he was the Polaroid artist who was plastered all over the Internet. That'd be interesting, if he was an artist. Perhaps he was the commune type. Cool. All the posts were about the same man, but when she searched images, she realized his picture didn't fit. He was only around thirty, this photographer guy. With limited time remaining, Abigail added "Becky Johnstone" to her father's name and location. Nothing, so she changed *Becky* to *Rebecca*.

The article flashed on screen only for a few seconds, but long enough for Abigail to discover that her father, ex-naval officer Grahame Johnston—married to actress Melanie Gallagher—was the managing director of a prebiotics company in Los Angeles. Long enough, also, for Abigail to zero in on the words she'd been searching for: *Daughter, Rebecca Johnstone, Age: 18.* The 3-D–throbbed in her eyes. Rebecca Johnstone: the daughter of an ex-naval officer. Rebecca Johnstone: just two years older than she was.

My sister.

She did exist. And Abigail had a letter and twenty-five thousand pounds to give her.

The plane was boarding. First class passengers boarded first. She had a window seat: 9A. Abigail wondered if this lump of metal would really fly. How could it possibly? A camp American of around twenty was seated next to her. He had dark blond hair, a little over-groomed in a mock-distressed kind of way, brown eyes, and an easy smile. "You been to LA before?" he asked, perhaps noticing her twitchiness.

"I've never been anywhere."

"You'll miss Scotland." The guy seemed nostalgic as he stared past her out the window.

She laughed. "I don't think so."

Abigail only relaxed her grip on the wide plastic arm rest

after the plane seemed to level off. Glasgow looked equally depressing from the air. Yellow lights, thick, dark un-majestic river, oppressive hood of ever-present cloud pushing down, down. And just like that, it was gone. She was *in* the clouds now. And above. On her way to this new life, whatever it would be. Over the next hour she wondered about the ground below her. Was she passing over Dunoon, where she grew up? As she wondered, she found herself humming a song Billy Connolly and the Humblebums wrote after the American navy left the town:

> *Has three pubs*
> *Two cafes*
> *And a fag machine*
> *And hills you can walk on*
> *While the rain is running doon*
> *. . . And a nightlife that stops in the afternoon*
> *Why don't they come back to Dunoon?*

So he was an ex-naval officer, her father. Abigail assumed he must have been stationed at Holy Loch in Dunoon, where the US nuclear submarines were based for thirty years. Perhaps her mother had been in the commune there at the time. Was it a Romeo/Juliet romance, perhaps? Forbidden, impossible? Hmm, romantic. The Americans eventually left Dunoon and the town collapsed too, its energy and livelihood gone with the submarines. That's where Abigail grew up: in a balloon with no air, in a dead seaside town, the only place on earth with more rain and less going for it than Glasgow.

Why had her father never known about her? Had he left before her mother knew she was pregnant? Did she ever try and tell him? Why had he taken two-year-old Becky?

Maybe tomorrow Abigail would ask her father all these questions. Or maybe she'd be so happy she wouldn't care. Maybe she would be thankful to know nothing about her past.

She pushed down the television screen in front of her. According to the map, they were flying over ocean, lots of it: a digital blue mass. Dunoon gone. Glasgow gone. Scotland gone. Ha, gone. She let out a big sigh. *My mother got me out of there*, she thought. *Thank you, Sophie Thom. Thank you, Mum.*

"You leaving someone behind?" the camp guy asked.

"Yeah," Abigail heard herself answer. She didn't bother to add that this someone was dead and that she hadn't even known her. It had struck her unexpectedly, the realization that she would never know her mother. Throughout her life, she had carried around with her the dream that her mother was out there somewhere; that even though Mum was a bitch from hell for abandoning her infant daughter, she existed. That dream had sometimes made her angry, sometimes sad, sometimes hopeful. Now it was gone.

"Here, what's your favorite drink?" the guy asked. He reached up and clicked the light for the stewardess to come. "We'll drink to our loved ones."

"Pineapple juice."

"Sure you don't want a gin and tonic? I hate drinking alone."

There are benefits to being a thirty-two-year-old Romanian called Alina, Abigail realized.

Moments later she found herself clinking glasses with her new friend, Bren ("short for Brendan, but call me that and I *will* kill you. Last name McDowell."). She sipped an icy lime-wedged first-class drink of gin and tonic.

"What have you done to your hair, girl?" Bren asked, after a few sips.

"Long story."

Before she knew it, Abigail found herself confessing. The truth, stripped down: dead mother, father and sister she never knew, the money, Billy and Camelia—the whole sordid lot. Abigail never usually opened up, especially not to boys. But Bren was utterly non-threatening. He hung on her every word. *He was easy on the eyes too,* she thought with a sigh, as so many gay men are: well dressed, pretty, approachable, perfect, and impossible. Besides, would she ever see him again? Probably not.

Fortunately, given his turn, Bren was also a talker. After the second round of drinks, Abigail sank back into the cushions and let him go. First came the tales of how his mother had gone to Canada to travel and fallen in love. A love refugee! His parents were both police officers, "but you'd never guess," he said. His father had been a "highly respected and very creative homicide detective, helping solve some of the most notorious cases in the country." (He said this part with a hint of mockery.) His mother worked in domestic violence and rape. They took early retirement and were now travelling the world

in a Winnebago. "Well, California. Next stop, Europe," Bren
slurred. "They're obsessed with conspiracy theories. If you ever
meet them, don't ask about 9/11."

Bren loved Scotland, everything about it, especially the
Tunnock's Tea Cakes. He came back as often as he could to
stay with the rellies in Partickhill. He'd recently moved from
Toronto to LA to make it in the movie business. "Not acting,
before you ask. Hair and makeup!" So far, all he'd managed was
a partnership in a salon. But he wouldn't give up, oh no.

He fell asleep mid-story.

Prebiotics sounds interesting, Abigail thought once he was
snoring. Her father was the managing director of a prebiotics
company. Managing director! He must be into science. Like
father, like daughter. He must be rich. Have power. Wear suits.
Tell hundreds of people what to do. Live in a mansion with a
pool. Have more than one car. Buy his kid and wife expensive
presents. Talk about prebiotics on the phone to the very people
who are helping him make the world better with prebiotics.
It was Abigail's new favorite word. She decided to nudge her
neighbor.

"Do you know what prebiotics is?"

"Huh?" Bren yawned and scrunched his eyebrows, rubbing
his chin. "Yeah, I know that . . . Prebiotics, I've heard of it."

Abigail suppressed a smile. She wanted to stop him there.
Bren obviously found it rude and impossible to admit that he
didn't have a clue. Must be the Glaswegian genes. Ask someone
from Glasgow to direct you to the railway station and they'll
send you anywhere rather than shrugging nowhere.

"I think it's like . . ." Bren continued. "You know how you have the Neanderthal period, right? And the post-Neanderthal period and then there's the pre-Neanderthal period?"

"Uh-huh."

"Well this is the same, I think. Except it's the period before the biotic one."

Abigail laughed. "That's ridiculous!"

"I'm ridiculous? Who cares? Get interesting, girl!" He closed his eyes and nestled into his pillow again, a playful grin on his lips.

"I'll try."

She grinned, too. She *would* see him again. In her new life, whatever that was, she'd have a friend waiting in Los Angeles.

SHE WOKE WHEN THE seatbelt sign came on. They were descending. The local time was 7:35 A.M. Panicked, Abigail rubbed her eyes and gaped out the window. It didn't look much different than Glasgow from up there. At least there were no clouds.

She was even more nervous waiting in line behind Bren to go through Immigration.

"Relax," Bren told her. "Stay cool. Don't worry so much! Or at least, don't let on."

A few questions later, Bren's passport was stamped. "You got my card?" he asked before heading to baggage claim.

"I have, yeah." She fished it out of her pocket and held it up.

"Call me."

"I will."

"I'll sort that hair!"

His glassy gaze met with hers. He didn't blink. He held on. Abigail swallowed and smiled back. He didn't care about her hair. He knew too much about the rest of her.

AT THE PASSPORT BOOTH, Abigail tried her best to look like normal, everyday thirty-two-year-old Romanian Alina Beklea. Underneath, she felt the same way she'd felt since Nieve died: powerless. She thought she'd made it. She thought the Glasgow airport was the one to worry about. She'd relaxed on the plane, gotten tipsy, blurted everything out to some guy she didn't even know, not realizing that she still might not make it to her new life.

The passport official was looking at the photograph.

Then he was looking at her.

She recognized the look. It was one of disdain. He thought she was scum. If there wasn't a problem, he wouldn't look at her like this. There was obviously a problem.

He looked at her, at the photograph, at her—again and again.

"You don't like Kate Middleton?" he asked with a nod to the STUFF THE MONARCHY shirt.

"Oh, well . . . I don't know her." Abigail faked a Romanian accent. "I just visited UK for a while."

"You have no visa."

"No, I didn't realize . . ." She lost the ability to breathe. *Visa?* The woman at the American Airlines desk hadn't checked or asked. "Can I get one?"

The glare he offered in return indicated that this was the dumbest question she could have possibly asked.

He called over a colleague. Both stared at the passport. Then they both gave her the same look of disdain.

"Come with us, please, Miss Beklea."

IN THE INTERVIEW ROOM, face-to-face with another sour man in a blue immigration uniform, Abigail went over the options in her head. She could run for it. The door was open. Outside the room was an empty corridor, equally as claustrophobic and fluorescent. If she ran to the left, she would reach the passport booth, where she'd come from. If she ran to the right, who knows where she'd end up? Scanning the room she was in and what she could see of the corridor, she noticed cameras. They were all over the ceilings. No: running was out.

She could cry. Girls in the hostel always cried when they wanted something. Abigail tried to muster a girly tear. No luck.

She could lie. Stick with the Alina story. Ask about getting a visa. Hell, beg. Or . . .

Bribe? But, no. Lies always caught up with you. And she doubted any amount of cash would convince the airport security authorities to let her through. Besides, she only had £1,570 of her £25,000 left. The other £25K was her sister's. She would never touch it.

Abigail clenched her jaw, angry with herself. She wasn't an impatient person. She shouldn't have rushed out of the country without thinking about the consequences. She should have found her father's address, contacted him, and explained her passport situation. She should have waited. There was no other option but to come clean to this dickhead.

"My father is Grahame Johnstone," she began. "I—"

"We'll be sending you straight back," he interrupted with no trace of sympathy. "Until we arrange it, wait here."

UNBELIEVABLE. SO CLOSE. A new life, just outside this room! A few yards away. And US Customs was sending her back to Glasgow. But she knew the reason. It wasn't because she was a liar. It was because she hadn't been meticulous enough. She hadn't fully established that new routine; she hadn't gone fully into that cold robot mode necessary to bluff her way past immigration officials at an international airport. She *could* have. A little more careful planning, a little more preparation. Instead, she'd allowed herself to get all excited and distracted. She'd helped Camelia escape. She'd gone to her mother's funeral. She'd gotten drunk on a plane with a gay guy. How stupid she had been to imagine a happy, sunny new place!

You are stupid, Abigail. You are stupid, stupid, stupid.

Maybe she should just go to the Solid Bar and do what Billy wanted her to do. Maybe the numbness of heroin would be better than the steady rain of disappointment . . .

She wasn't sure how long she'd been sitting in the cold plastic chair in the interview room, head in her knees—maybe an hour—when a different man burst through the door.

He was tall, straight-backed, suited, shoes so shiny they hurt her eyes. He oozed significance. "So you're Grahame Johnstone's daughter?" he barked.

"Yes?"

"Get up. Follow me." The voice was presidential, the kind you know you have to stop and listen to, then obey.

Abigail picked up her backpack and followed. She couldn't concentrate on anything but her feet—one foot ahead of the other—just behind those shiny black shoes. They passed through a doorway.

The man stopped. "Here she is," he said. His tone suddenly softened.

After Abigail dared to look up, she found herself in another office, very similar to the one she'd just left. Or perhaps it was the same one. Could be. Same size, same table, same three chairs. The only difference was that there were no immigration officials, only a middle-aged man in a golfing get-up.

"Hello, Abigail." The golfer held out his hand. "I'm your father."

CHAPTER FOUR

While her father wasn't dead, the reunion didn't feel very different from when she'd met her dead mother. Grahame Johnstone seemed eager to make physical contact with the handshake. But Abigail couldn't move.

"I'm sorry, Abigail." His arm fell aside. "This is a bit awkward."

Tiny relief: he hadn't presumed to call her Abi. But if he had, she wouldn't have challenged him. This man was her father. Her *father*. The word was as terrifying and nonsensical as *visa*. Nieve had told her more than once: *"Just think of your father as a sperm donor."* There had been times when she'd fantasized about a dad, mostly that first year when Jason McVeigh still thought adoption might be a possibility. The few times she'd indulged herself since, she'd imagined a rugged Irish movie star like Liam Neeson: the kind of man who saves the world against all odds, but saves his daughter first—as his daughter is much, much more important to him than the world.

The man in front of her was not Liam Neeson. He was

stern, sensible, reliable: the kind of guy who plays the second husband in a romantic comedy, the boring one for whom the feisty wife leaves the flawed-but-lovable first husband. Abigail scrutinized his features. He did look familiar, something about his eyes. So strange, like seeing a famous person in the street and assuming you know them. She didn't know him, but he was . . . he was . . . *my God.* His eyes were the same color and shape as hers. And his lips went lopsided when he smiled, down to the left, just like hers did.

"Look at you," he said. "I'm sorry. I guess I'm not so sure how to handle this. The last thing I want to do is freak you out."

Freak me out? She started to melt. "About the passport . . ." Abigail realized she needed to explain herself. "I didn't have one of my own, see. Had to buy one. I should have waited to do it officially, but I was in a rush—"

"It's okay. They're not sending you back. You're not in trouble."

Her gaze narrowed. "I'm not?"

"I pulled some strings," he said.

"Pulled some strings?" she repeated.

"Don't worry about it."

At last, Abigail felt relief. Blessed relief. She wouldn't be going back to Glasgow. But then she found herself wondering how the hell a person, no matter how powerful, could get a virtual stranger past International Customs. *He is a clever man,* her mother had written. Thinking about it now, it didn't read like a compliment. Clever might equal cunning. Clever might equal sinister: a gangster or corrupt politician. It might equal anything. And it was very clear that her mother didn't want her father knowing about either the letter or the money. But she did mention he was kind, and to accept his kindness . . .

"Do you have any other luggage?" he asked.

"No, this is it." She nervously patted the backpack on her shoulders.

He flashed another lopsided smile. "Well then, let's get out of here, okay?"

THE WALK TO THE car only took ten minutes. Neither she nor her father spoke. She was a fast walker, Abigail. Not a stroller. Her legs took her places—usually not very nice places before now—but she'd always thought of them as pure transport. She was slow compared to her father, who walked at breakneck speed. She practically had to run to keep up with him.

His car was a grey Audi convertible, roof down. Backpack in the backseat, they drove out of the airport and made their way onto the freeway.

Okay. She could breathe. This wasn't a dream. She'd done it. She'd escaped.

The sun was shining on her face! The loud wind was rushing through her hair!

She closed her eyes and breathed in LA. *Hmm*, it smelled . . . like car fumes.

Her lashes fluttered open. Yes, she was still nervous about the man at the wheel, this Grahame Johnstone father of hers who pulled strings and drove soft-tops. His beige golf trousers and short-sleeved white shirt certainly fit the corrupt politician idea. How old was he? Around forty? Had all his hair, a kind of flat brown that looked artificial. Was it a wig? Did he dye it? Maybe it was acceptable for a man to dye his hair in LA. In Glasgow, you'd be shot. His glasses had a label on the side. She couldn't make out what it said, but she could tell they were expensive. And they made him look clever. That word again: *clever.* Most of all, he seemed too straight for Sophie Thom. Even in death, she had some kind of edge.

Also: what should she call him?

She repeated the possibilities in her head: *Dad, Grahame, Father, Daddy, Oh-Daddy-my-Daddy, Mr. Johnstone.* Looking sideways as subtly as she could, she noticed that his brown eyes were always flitting from left to right.

Finally he spoke. "We're going to meet Becky for breakfast. That okay?"

It was. She was starving, but more importantly, she was dying to meet her sister. She hoped it would feel less complicated than meeting *him.* She hadn't expected anything—perhaps because she hadn't had enough time to think about it—but she didn't like how she felt. Uncomfortable questions multiplied like a virus in her head. A powerful stranger was now her custodian. He was driving her to his home, where she would stay. He was so very different from the crazy rebel he'd married all those years ago. His shirt had no creases. He smelled clean: not perfumed, but of soap and fresh air. He was alien, like no man she had ever encountered. Abigail wondered for a moment if he was real. Next time she turned to look at him, perhaps he would pull his face off to reveal a lizard head underneath. For a brief, panicky second, Abigail pictured herself jumping out of the car at the next red light—

"Bit of a drive first." His voice stopped the racing thoughts. She felt she should say something like: "Is it?" But she didn't want to waste time. No use engaging in idle conversation. She wanted to get to know him. She wanted to stop feeling worried and suspicious. Also, she wanted him to like her, and people who are *interested* are likable. It might not work out, this father-daughter/family thing, but she needed to make it as smooth as possible. For at least a year . . . by which time she would be seventeen and familiar with this new world. She could go it alone after that. So there was no point in delaying the important questions: Why had he suddenly appeared in her life? How had he rescued her at the airport?

"So, tell me about your company," she began. "Prebiotics, yeah?"

He smiled faintly, his eyes on the road. "Oh, you know about that?"

"I Googled you."

"Ah." Grahame's *Ah* had a slightly worried tone to it. Snapping out of it, he said, "GJ Prebiotics is the name. Five years in business. It's big, what we're doing."

"I don't know what prebiotics are . . . is."

"Oh, well, that's not unusual. It's very new."

Can't be that new, she almost said. *Five years in business, right?*

Now they were heading off the freeway onto actual streets,

where she could make out actual buildings. So far, LA was not particularly appealing. Abigail could just see the distant outline of glassy high-rises through the smog, above a sea of low-lying buildings, each different from the next in its own unspectacular way. Signs swooped by overhead: BOWL! MCDONALD'S! FREEWAY ENTRANCE! OPENING SOON! SORRY WE'RE CLOSED! She knew there were hills here somewhere, but couldn't see any. DO NOT ENTER! TACO BELL! GRINDER! MCDONALD'S (again)!

She made a wish that her new home would be on top of an invisible hill. The city seemed soulless. That wasn't something you could criticize Glasgow for. One thing it did have was soul.

"Prebiotics are not the same as probiotics, which you *will* know about," her father said.

"Oh." Abigail shrugged and smiled awkwardly.

"Okay, well you know those yogurt drinks you see advertised on the TV? 'Yakult, for a healthy gut!'"

"Uh-huh."

"They're probiotics. They help maintain the natural balance of organisms in the intestines. The normal human digestive tract contains about four hundred types of probiotic bacteria that reduce the growth of harmful bacteria and promote a healthy digestive system."

"Right." *Just a typical father-daughter reunion conversation,* she thought.

"But that's not prebiotics."

"Oh." Sweet Lord, there was more.

"Prebiotics help probiotics to work, if you take them first."

"So . . . you make yogurt drinks?" She didn't want to let on, but her flat voice had already given the anticlimax away. A fucking yogurt drink. Not *even* a yogurt drink. The drink you take in order to take a yogurt drink. The conversation wasn't helping her work him out at all. He could be anyone, or anything. There was no other option; she would have to be more direct.

"I hope you don't mind me asking, but how do you pull strings?"

He chewed his lip, his grip tightening on the steering wheel.

Okay, so he was her father, but that didn't really mean anything, not yet anyway. "How'd you get me through customs even though I had a phony passport?"

"I paid," he said with a sigh. He turned to flash a disarming smile, benign and genuine. "There are very few things money can't buy."

Abigail felt another wave of guilty relief. *Don't I know it,* she thought. "How much?" she asked.

He laughed and turned back to the road ahead. "You know what? I think you are going to get on very well with your sister."

ALMOST AS SOON AS they sat at an outside table, Grahame's mobile phone went off. He answered in a very serious voice and said nothing but "uh-huh" and "yes." When he hung up, it rang again. He didn't apologize before answering, and once more embarked on a similarly boring monosyllabic conversation.

Abigail took in the world around her as he busied himself on the phone. The bright yellow restaurant was opposite a palm-tree-lined beach. Just as she'd imagined: people dressed in colors other than black, with faces other than white, walking, cycling, running, and rollerblading on the boardwalk.

Grahame finally hung up again. "Sorry about that." He glanced at his watch. "We're a bit early. It's nine fifty. I told Becky ten o'clock. You want a drink? Juice or water?"

She shrugged. "Pineapple juice'd be good."

"Shall we order?"

Abigail bit her lip as she scanned the menu. She had only eaten in a restaurant twice before: both times with disgruntled care workers watching her every move; both times at cheap, cheerless chain-restaurant Nando's; both times she had been asked to choose the cheapest thing on the menu (3x chicken wings, £3). Abigail didn't want breakfast. She'd lost track of what time it was in the UK. But her body told her she needed food. Besides, she'd imagined eating salad in her new dream world, so why not? The house salad seemed pretty cheap, if dollars were still less than pounds.

"Just the salad, ta."

Her father ordered a bacon roll.

"Got hooked on these in Dunoon," he said as the waiter left with their order.

Dunoon. Our shared past! She was about to ask him about it when he looked over his shoulder and announced: "And here she is."

Abigail did not believe in ghosts. Many dark, boring hours had been filled playing with Ouija boards in shelters and foster homes. While she'd screamed a couple of times at the moving letters that spelled things like "death to Colin" (one of the social workers), she never really bought any of it. But when she turned and saw her sister for the first time, Abigail found herself staring at the undead. It was Sophie Thom with twenty years sucked out and fresh life blown in. This girl—this young Winona Ryder with short cropped dark hair, with a petite silver nose and belly button ring (visible under the crop top)—was the spitting image of Mum.

"Oh my God," Abigail whispered out loud, accidentally.

"You must be my little sister," her dead mother said.

"I . . ." She couldn't string a sentence together

"Are you okay?" Grahame asked. "This must be a lot to take in."

Abigail took a deep breath, tried to shake off the shock, and stood up to face her sister. There was an aura, an energy, about this girl. Her eyes buzzed. "I'm sorry, it's just you look—"

"Identical to Sophie," Becky interrupted lightly. "So I hear."

"Freakishly so." Abigail swallowed. Her eyes began to sting. The exhaustion was finally catching up with her. Here she was with a father who looked like her and a sister who looked like her mother. *This must be what a "family" is*, she thought to herself. A group of people who have indisputable, physical proof that they belong together.

Becky held out her hand to shake Abigail's. "I'm so pleased to meet you."

Abigail took her sister's hand for a trembling shake. Before she knew what was happening, Becky had hauled her in for a hug.

"I'm so, so glad you're here," Becky whispered in her ear. "I mean it, Abigail." Her voice quavered. "You have no idea."

ABIGAIL YEARNED FOR A moment alone, to take it all in. She sat crumpled in her chair, unable to speak. All she could think was that if she'd lived a privileged life, she'd probably be even *more* like her father. She'd have done physics and chemistry, for a start. She'd have had a room of her own, a desk to study on, and would have topped all her classes. Right now, she'd be getting ready for the next step, university. Hell, she'd probably be wearing slacks and a cardigan.

These thoughts suddenly made her aware of her STUFF THE MONARCHY T-shirt. Her father seemed to notice her attempt to zip up her jacket.

"So, you don't like Kate Middleton?"

"Oh, well, I've never met her . . . of course. I'm sorry. I suppose it's a little—"

"The Scots hate the English, Dad," Becky said. "You should know that."

He blinked and tried to smile. "Sorry. I'm nervous, making small talk. Do you think Scotland will be independent one day, Abigail?"

"Maybe, I don't know." She finally managed to close the zipper even though she had never been so hot in her life (and it was still morning!). She thought the Royals were a bunch of tosspots, but not because of Scottish nationalism. Just as nicknames were for people who were loved, nationalism was for people who belonged.

"I *love* your accent! Say 'Ach aye the noo'!" Becky demanded.

"Sorry?"

"'Ach aye the noo!' You know, Scottish for 'Oh yes, right now'!"

"Ach aye the noo?" Abigail was confused. She'd never heard or said anything of the sort.

Becky clapped her hands and laughed. "I hate my accent. You are so lucky. So, Dad phoned and told me what was happening at the airport. I was very impressed! I take it the makeup was part of the disguise?"

Abigail had forgotten about the green eye shadow and inch-thick foundation. She touched her cheek, embarrassed.

"Here, use one of these to get it off." Becky grabbed a small packet of makeup wipes from her bag and handed it to her. It took six wipes and an agonizing three minutes to remove the gunk Camelia had plastered there. Grahame kept pulling his phone out of his pocket and glancing at it the whole time. "Hello, there you are!" Becky said when the makeup was all gone. "Wow. You don't need to wear any ever. Gorgeous."

The food arrived, thankfully. Abigail wasn't used to being complimented.

Her eyes widened. Her plate was huge, bright and beautiful, a salad unlike any she'd ever seen. Since leaving the commune, eating was not one of Abigail's pleasures. She hated doing it in front of people. She picked out tiny pieces of lettuce nervously, making sure they were small enough to get into her mouth in one bite.

Her father, on the other hand, was a comfortable eater. Not

nervous about spillages, like she was. Crumbs of bacon fell from his chin as he devoured the roll.

Becky wasn't hungry. Maybe she'd already eaten, because she didn't order anything. As Abigail negotiated the greens, her sister started talking.

"What do you think of LA?"

She had to chew for several seconds before being able to swallow and answer. "It's big."

"Does it always rain in Glasgow?"

"Yes."

Nice easy questions, all of them, but chewing and anxiety made it difficult to answer. In the end, Abigail asked if she should get a doggy bag. "I'm not as hungry as I thought I was."

"Just leave it." Her father's kind smile made her cringe.

I'm a fool, aren't I? she thought. She already knew the answer. There was too much to learn.

BECKY LINKED HER ARM through Abigail's as they walked to their cars, almost as if sensing Abigail needed a crutch. "Did he tell you all about his prebiotics?"

"He did."

"Fascinating stuff, eh." Then she whispered: "Just his day job."

Abigail didn't have time to ask her what she meant. They'd reached Becky's van. It was beat-up, a jalopy—a stark contrast to their father's car.

"We'll follow you," Grahame stated. He nodded toward his passenger seat.

Abigail wanted to ride with Becky, but she sensed it wasn't up for discussion. She slid in beside Grahame and buckled up. They followed behind Becky out of the airport, onto a freeway, and then up into the hills. The streets got leafier, the houses bigger, the wind cooler. Abigail found herself grinning. Movie stars probably lived here. She wondered if she'd spot any, then chastised herself for being so shallow. A few minutes later, Grahame clicked a button on the dashboard. A large iron gate on the side of a winding road began to open. They turned right into a circular driveway. Another button made the garage doors open. Grahame drove inside and pressed yet another button that made the roof close over.

Amazing: a world controlled by buttons. *In robot mode, I'll fit right in.*

Abigail closed the door and looked at her father. "Thanks..." she started. *Oh Jesus*, she had to call him something.

"I'd like it if you called me Dad. If you want to, that is." He'd read her thoughts. He was a mind-reading lizard alien. Not like in *The Shining*, though; she certainly couldn't read his.

She bit her lip and nodded across the car at him, knowing she should repeat the word. It wasn't a hard thing to do, after all. *Repeat the word. Just do it.*

"Thanks, Dad." She couldn't get out of the garage fast enough.

The place was built with spotless blond stone, bay windows, and Greek style columns. Two stories high and at least four rooms wide, it lorded over the immaculate garden like a Glasgow mansion on steroids.

Becky hooked Abigail's arm again as they walked from the garage to the main entrance. A young woman was waiting for them.

"That's the Stepford Wife," Becky whispered.

"Abigail, this is Melanie," Grahame introduced. "Melanie, this is Abigail."

Melanie smiled and gave Abigail a short hug. It wasn't hard to reciprocate, as Abigail felt nothing toward this woman. She wasn't a relative. She was a random factor in this bizarre equation, but not at all threatening. She certainly *seemed* uncomplicated; her smile was warm, and her clothes were almost old-fashioned: fifties-style, pastel, pretty. She was a lot younger than Grahame—about thirty—with hazel eyes and perfect shoulder-length blonde hair.

"You are so pretty!" Melanie withdrew from the embrace, holding Abigail's shoulders to study her. "Look at you! Just like your father. Your eyes! Can you see it, Grahame? She's *you*! Come in, Abigail; come inside your new home!"

CHAPTER FIVE

They're staring at me. I must look like a freak.

In the last two days, Abigail had negotiated a non-stop barrage of the alien and unknown: hospital, crematorium, airport, soft-top car, impossibly large salad . . . nothing out of the ordinary for most people; everything out of the ordinary for a Glasgow street punk. Now, sitting in this vast living room as this stunning woman poured tea for the four of them, she realized she was shaking. The cup rattled against the saucer. She'd never had tea made in a pot before. She'd never drunk tea out of a cup before. Mugs, always mugs. Stained ones. The cup and saucer shared a blue floral pattern. The china was almost see-through. It must have cost a fortune. Grahame and Becky sipped from their armchairs, unable to mask their concern.

"Are you all right, dear?" Melanie asked.

She quickly set the cup on the glass table. She clasped her hands together to steady herself. "I'm fine. I'm just a little . . ."

"Jet-lagged?" Melanie finished for her. "Don't apologize!

Crossing nine time zones wreaks havoc on the system! It'll be a few days before your sleep cycle gets back to normal."

Abigail smiled. Melanie might as well have spoken in Romanian. Fortunately, perky new Stepmom went back to talking about the renovations she'd just completed. *This room used to have dark brown carpet! Dark brown! Getting the chimney sorted was a nightmare!* Abigail tried to nod politely, but she couldn't bring herself to meet the curious gazes. Her eyes wandered toward the adjoining library. Through the door, she could see the polished wooden shelves reaching to the ceiling with gorgeous leather-bound books. In the corner was an old fashioned gramophone. The bookcase behind it was stuffed with paper-covered records.

"Oh, the library renovation was your dad's project," Melanie said.

"I take it someone's into vinyl?" Abigail asked.

"I collect seventy-eights," Grahame explained. "My hobby."

Abigail didn't know what seventy-eights were. If she asked, she had a sense her father might talk about it for hours. She changed the subject to something more important. "So, if you don't mind my asking, what about school?"

"Becky went to boarding school in England," Grahame said. "Rodean."

Abigail's heart sank. She'd heard of Rodean. Poshest girls' school in the kingdom. In bloody England! Anyone who went there, no matter where they came from, ended up speaking like the Queen. Feck, they were going to send her back to the UK. She'd end up in a dormitory with a bunch of Sloane's who buy pre-wrapped gifts at Harrods with daddy's credit card.

"I was expelled," Becky said.

Grahame almost choked on some tea. "It wasn't right for Becky."

Abigail couldn't help but smile. Score one for her new sister.

"No, it wasn't for me," Becky said, smiling back conspiratorially.

"So, I phoned Frank Henderson at Marlborough yesterday," Grahame concluded. "It's the best girls' school in LA. Obviously it's the summer break now, so you have three weeks to get yourself organized."

Thank God. Abigail's hands finally stopped trembling. She wasn't going back to the UK. She was staying right here in sunny California. No more need for phony passports or scary customs. And to top it all off, she'd be well educated. She *would* go to university.

"It's only a five-minute drive for you," Grahame added.

"Oh! But I can't drive."

"We can sort that out. Melanie, can you arrange things?"

"Of course," Melanie said. "You can start Driver's Ed and take a car service in the meantime. You'll have your license by Thanksgiving."

"You could get a van like mine!" Becky sounded excited. If Abigail had the choice she'd go for something very different, something with no roof perhaps.

"Or you could go for a soft top like mine?" Her father was still reading her thoughts. "Get some sun on that Scottish skin. What sort of car would you like?"

What sort of car would I like? She almost laughed at the

absurdity of the question. "I don't know. You don't have to get me one, you know."

"What about something pink?" Melanie suggested. Everyone in her new family seemed to have very firm ideas about cars.

"Think about it." Grahame put his tea cup down and slapped his hands on his knees. "I feel terrible about this, but I have to go to work. I'll be home for dinner though. Will you be all right?"

Abigail nodded. "Sure."

He stood and leaned down toward her. She wasn't sure why at first, but as he got closer she realized he was coming in for a hug. "Welcome home."

It wasn't easy hugging a standing man. She got it all wrong: put her arms under his, so hers landed around his waist, which felt ickily intimate. Plus, because she was sitting, her face was in his chest. She could barely get the words out—"Thanks, Dad"—before patting his back like boys do in order to stop the hug, to stop it right now.

He kissed Melanie then rubbed the top of Becky's head. "Your sister'll look after you. You wouldn't believe how excited she's been since she found out."

Becky shrugged. She caught Abigail's eyes. Her smile grew strained. She removed her father's hand and straightened her ruffled hair.

"Bye, my three lovely girls," he said, as if he'd said it all his life.

MELANIE SPENT THE NEXT half hour talking about the wel-
come-home event she was planning in Abigail's honor. *The
party of the season! The talk of the town! So much to do!*

Abigail's stomach twisted. The party felt wrong, and not
just because she was embarrassed at all the fuss. If her mother's letter was to be trusted, Grahame hadn't even known
she'd existed until a few days ago. And now her new stepmom
was planning a homecoming? On the other hand, her dead-
stranger-mother had written that her alive-stranger-father
would be kind to her. Clearly his kindness extended to the
alive-stranger-father's new wife. A party was certainly kind, if
it was anything.

You look like a size six! I know just the shop!

She liked Melanie, but she was talking too much.

What do the Scotch eat?

Scots! The Scots!

All the men should wear kilts—

"I'm going to show Abigail her room," Becky interrupted.

"Thanks for the tea, Melanie," Abigail called as her sister
dragged her out into the hall. "Thanks for everything!"

"HERE, HAVE SOME OF this, it'll loosen us up."

Abigail didn't smoke dope. Didn't like the feel of smoking,
for a start, but most of all, she hated losing control. She never
did that, ever. Now was definitely *not* the time to experiment.

When that blue Toyota drove her to a place called "care,"
everything was taken away except the clarity of her thoughts.
She'd clung to that clarity like a life raft ever since.

Besides, of all the newness to take in, the hardest was this ghost girl sitting cross-legged on the desk across from her. Even the pot smelled different, grown in the Californian sun and not under Scottish lamps, perhaps; or maybe it was the tobacco mixed in. Becky smoked like an old-fashioned movie star, unaware or unashamed. She could hold a joint, inhale and exhale while doing a host of other things, talking and sipping water, whatever the moment called for.

"No ta, it doesn't agree with me," Abigail said.

Becky studied her face. "It calms me down. I don't do anything else, but I love this stuff. We don't look alike, do we?" She blew the smoke out the open window. "You look like him. Your eyes. But you must have some of her. You're much better-looking than he is. Mind you, he was cute when he was young." She took another drag. "He was so different when he was young."

Abigail had been sitting with her legs crossed, too, but it was getting uncomfortable. She dangled her legs over the side of the desk and leaned back on her arms.

"You don't talk much." Becky's smile widened.

An answer wasn't required, so Abigail didn't offer one. She looked around the room. It was a mess, papers and clothes all over the floor. There was another desk with two computers on it. The floor was covered in files, paints, cardboard, and other art materials.

"Are you a happy person?" Becky asked.

Oh please, not stoner talk, Abigail groaned to herself. "How would I know?"

Becky laughed and took a sip of her bottled sparkling water. "You're happy then."

Abigail raised her eyebrows.

"You don't notice being happy," Becky offered. "You notice being unhappy." She giggled. "I'm sorry. I say a lot of dumb stuff that I think sounds profound."

Abigail laughed in spite of herself. "So what do you do with yourself, other than smoke?"

Becky rested the joint on a posh china saucer and took another sip of water. "Hmm. Well, Dad wanted me to study law. That was an argument!" She picked up the joint again, inhaled, exhaled, and then stared into Abigail's eyes. "I don't want to be stuck-up, play the game." Becky's face was too close to hers now, getting more and more intense. "See, I believe in freedom of expression. I believe that most old, rich folk should be shot. Especially if they tell young, poor kids that it's their fault they're poor. I believe in having fire in your belly." She pounded her flat stomach. "No one should be allowed to extinguish that, no one."

Abigail sighed. The rant took her back to the commune on Sunday evenings, when Nieve and her friends would take turns to address the community from a large wooden box on the loch side. Such passion seemed just a wee bit misplaced here with this privileged girl, in her posh room in her posh house, smoking a joint and drinking bottled water that probably cost more than a pint at the Solid Bar. But maybe a lot of Nieve's friends had come from privilege, too. She'd never stopped to think about it.

Becky stubbed out the joint and gestured to the art materials scattered around the room. "I'm an artist." She blushed. "Oh, jeez—that sounded so pretentious, didn't it?"

"No."

"What do you believe in?"

Bollocks. This is the conversation her sister wanted want to have? Now Abigail was pissed. Becky had no idea about poverty. She hadn't lived in a hostel filled with heroin addicts and prostitutes. This was all naïve and clichéd.

"You're kinda scary!" Becky exclaimed loudly.

Abigail sighed again, more loudly than she meant. Not only was this naïve and clichéd, it was irritatingly familiar. In No Life Hostel, the girls would smoke dope in the bathroom and get all weirded out by each other.

"Tell me what you believe in," Becky asked again.

Abigail bit her lip.

Becky laughed uncomfortably. "You're freaking me out. Say something!"

"It's just the dope."

"It's not. I don't mean to be rude, but you're so guarded. Anything, anything. Quick, before I explode."

The ghost is stoned. Now was not the time to share her questions about their dead mother. Nor about why their dead mother might want to keep their living father in the dark about the letter. Nor was it the time to talk about the letter itself, or about the £25,000 she had for Becky.

So Abigail said this instead: "I believe in survival. Is my room the one opposite this?"

—

BECKY DIDN'T FOLLOW HER, thankfully.

Abigail closed the door and leaned against it, shutting her eyes for a moment. When she glanced around, she saw a huge king-sized bed with way too many pillows. She also saw her very own bathroom. And a double window with sumptuous floral curtains overlooking the back garden, complete with a kidney-shaped swimming pool like the ones she'd seen through the windows of travel agencies. Well, of course there was a pool: it was so hot, at least thirty degrees Celsius. She'd never experienced temperatures above twenty-five. She took her leather jacket off and gazed at the pool. She was dying to cool down in it.

She guessed it was Melanie who had put an awful lot of effort into the room. Melanie was a willing servant of Grahame. And that was fine. The bedside table was stacked with lotions and potions. Melanie had placed a soft pink dressing gown on the bed and hung three prints of Scottish landscapes on the walls, probably to make her new stepdaughter feel at home.

Before she even knew what she was doing, Abigail took the prints down and slipped them under the bed. The last thing she wanted was to be reminded of that dump.

She ran her fingers over the soft covers and looked at herself in the mirror of the oak dresser. A pale, haggard girl stared back. But the girl was giddy, too. Forget the smiling reflection; what about that pristine glass? It was polished to an unreal shine. Abigail stifled a squeal. So what if her mother had secrets she didn't want her father to know about? People with money were strange, her mother included, clearly. She'd learn to adjust.

Wrapping herself in the thick feather duvet on the bed, she laughed and drifted off.

CHAPTER SIX

Knock knock.

What was that?

Knock knock.

Where was she?

"I'm coming in!" a voice said. Abigail rubbed her eyes and looked around. Fluffy duvet. Pillows. Private bathroom. Floral curtains, still open. Dark outside. *That's right,* she remembered. *I'm on a different planet now.* She smiled groggily.

"Dinner time." The voice was Becky's, who was in the bathroom turning on the shower. "Jump in, get dressed. Do you need some clothes?"

"Yeah, thanks."

The shower (like everything else) was the Priciest Mother-Shower brought down from Priciest Planet-Shower to hurt fair-skinned Scots who'd only ever experienced a feeble dribbling. Blimey, Americans did things properly.

"Clothes on the bed!" Becky yelled. "See ya down there!"

When Abigail had dried herself with the impossibly fluffy

towels, she put on the high-waisted denim shorts Becky had left for her, and then braved another glance in the mirror. She'd never worn shorts before. Her legs were blindingly white. The T-shirt was black, with a painting on the front of a bunch of faceless teenagers who looked like zombies. At the bottom of the painting was the letter "G." The initial of the brand, or artist, she supposed. *Whatever.*

The formal dining room was adjacent to the large dining kitchen at the back of the house. Her new family sat waiting for her, sipping red wine from round glasses so large that each could take a full bottle. Melanie and Grahame had changed into suave evening outfits. Becky had swapped her crop top for the same T-shirt Abigail now wore. Somehow, it looked much better on Becky. A wave of embarrassment overwhelmed her as she walked toward them with wet hair, bare legs and no shoes. "Sorry, I fell asleep and I only have these big boots."

"Don't apologize." Grahame opened his linen napkin and flattened it on his lap. "Jet lag's a killer."

Melanie had made chicken tikka masala "to make you feel at home!"

"Isn't that Indian?" Becky gasped. The chili caught in her throat.

"It is, but it's the most popular dish in the country. Big Indian/Pakistani community." Abigail stifled a cough as she shoved the food in her mouth. Melanie must have put at least a dozen of the burny beasts in the curry. She took a breath, wiped the sweat from her forehead and swallowed a large piece of leathery chicken. "That was right thoughtful, thanks Melanie."

"Sorry, what was that?"

Abigail blinked nervously. Had she said something wrong? "I said that was right thoughtful of you, the curry and all."

Melanie patted her hand against her chest and laughed. "It's your accent! God willing it'll soften after a while. I'll catch every lovely little thing you say."

Abigail made a mental note to practice an American accent. The quicker she got rid of her rough brogue, the better. After the ordeal of the main course came burnt caramel shortbread which Melanie had baked "to make you feel at home!" Conversation was polite, and all about the party. Melanie had spent the day making arrangements. It would be tomorrow night. Everything would be Scotch.

Scottish!

"I'll get you a dress for the party and some other clothes in the morning." Melanie shot a hard glare at Abigail's T-shirt. "I see Becky gave you one of *those*. Do we know if it even means anything yet?"

"Pardon?" Abigail asked, lost.

Grahame took it upon himself to explain. "I'm sure you don't know anything about this, Abigail, coming from a more civilized continent." (She couldn't tell if he was joking or not.) "For the past month, there's been a graffiti campaign here in LA. The images are the same as those on your T-shirts. Rumor has it there's one letter to go. It's become a kind of cult. Sad to say, the more susceptible teens of LA, like Becky here, have subscribed to it." He cast a sidelong glance at his daughter. "The press has called it 'The Graffiti Tease.' To me, it looks like an advertising campaign—probably building up to launch some kid's amateur homemade zombie movie or something. In my honest opinion, though, it's just vandalism, pure and simple."

For the first time, Abigail saw some passion in her father's eyes. The subject of graffiti had eroded his guard. She liked that something upset him. It made him more real.

"It's freedom of expression," Becky said, staring back at him.

Abigail suddenly wished she'd worn her STUFF THE MON-ARCHY T-shirt instead. She wanted to remain invisible here. Political protest in the UK seemed to be a less contentious issue than vandalism in LA. Fine by her. She had no political allegiances whatsoever.

"I'll get you some new clothes tomorrow," Melanie said, ever the peacemaker.

"I have plenty of clothes for Abigail," Becky said. "We're sisters, you know. They'll probably fit." Her tone was flat.

Grahame and Melanie glanced at each other.

"I hope you don't mind," Grahame said. He wiped his mouth with his serviette, folded it neatly, and placed it beside his empty dessert bowl. "We have drinks tonight with our good friends, the Howards. Planned it ages ago. We'd take you, but—"

"You'd be bored out of your brain," Becky finished.

He smirked. "Well, yes, frankly. Becky will look after you."

"But I'm going out, too. *I* planned it ages ago," Becky protested.

"Take Abigail. I'm sure she'd love to go."

"It won't be fun for her."

Abigail swallowed. They were suddenly talking about her as if she weren't in the room. Bad sign. It was the same thing social workers always did whenever she was about to be moved.

"Becky, it's your sister's first night here." Grahame's voice hardened. "Either don't go out or take her with you."

"It's your *daughter's* first night here," Becky snarled, grabbing her dishes in a huff and storming off to the kitchen.

ABIGAIL COULDN'T CARE LESS about going out. She didn't want to tag along with Becky. Mostly she wanted to snoop around the house, alone. But she did hate the fact that she was already a nuisance. It was clear Becky resented her. Who wouldn't? A brand-new sister: a crazy street punk with a stupid accent who had stormed into Becky's cozy existence without warning. All her life, Abigail had worked hard at not getting in people's way, at not *needing* people, and here she was on the very first day, already a needy pain in the ass.

The moment Melanie and Grahame left the two of them alone—not before hugging Abigail again (she hoped all this demonstrativeness would peter out)—Becky dashed upstairs. Abigail followed to find her in the hall, pulling down a ladder from a trapdoor in the ceiling.

"Listen, I'll stay here," Abigail told her. "I'll be fine."

"No. I've been told." Becky climbed up the ladder and disappeared into the attic space.

The curt martyr-tone was too much. "I don't want to come," Abigail snapped.

Her sister appeared at the trapdoor. "Come up and grab the bottom of this."

Abigail knew she couldn't argue. It was too soon. And judging from Becky's smile, Becky also knew that she was in total control of the situation. Abigail climbed to the top, where her new sister was gripping the edge of a large chest, ready to descend.

"Grab the other end. Can you slide it down? It's not heavy."

"No problem," Abigail muttered.

The chest felt empty. Nothing rattled inside. It bumped against each rung of the ladder as she backed herself down and slid it onto the floor.

"I found it up there last week," Becky said when she reached the hall floor. "Might break it open and use it for storage."

"What's up there?"

"Just a bunch of old junk. Sentimental stuff he's hidden away."

"Is he very sentimental?"

"Okay, wrong word. I'd describe Dad as . . . misguided. Ha! That's what he says about me." Becky slid the ladder back into place. "About tonight. Can you keep your mouth shut?"

"Depends."

"You have to promise me you will."

Abigail felt herself slump. Would this involve pissing off her dad and Melanie? Or something illegal that could send her back to Glasgow? "Like I said, I'd actually prefer to stay here. I'll stay in my room and tell them you took me."

"No. Come on." Becky sighed. "Look, I'm sorry I got bitchy. But you have to promise to keep your mouth shut."

"Not if your secret involves hurting anyone."

Becky's eyes flickered, as if she were offended. "Really?"

"Yeah, *really*."

"It won't hurt anyone."

"Or get me in trouble?"

"You'll be fine." Becky hesitated. "Abigail, I'm glad you're here. I mean it. I want you to do this with me."

Abigail thought for a moment. "Okay then." To be honest, she was dying to know what on earth her sister was up to that required strict codes of secrecy and this empty chest. She helped her sister carry it downstairs, stopping to rest in the hall.

"What's in there?" Abigail pointed to a closed door, wondering what the rules were in a family home like this. Did door closed mean never go in; or knock first, then go in? (Becky had entered her room with just a preliminary knock.) It struck Abigail as she looked around that this was the first time she'd ever had an *exact* address. If someone wrote to her, they'd address the letter to this exact place, not "C/O Peace Camp" or "C/O Glasgow City Council." It wasn't a van. And it wasn't a shared shitehole. In the former, there was only one door, always unlocked, and she couldn't recall ever knocking on it. In the latter, all the doors were fire resistant, with rectangles of reinforced glass. Entering them always required permission and was always done with a certain amount of trepidation. Here, there were dozens of them, all safe and open and welcoming and *hers*. Except for two: Becky's bedroom and this one off the hall.

"It's his den," Becky finally said. "The torture chamber! Let's get out of here."

After some more grunting and groaning, Abigail managed to load the trunk into the back of her sister's van, amidst piles of things (who knows what?) that were covered in blankets. She shut the passenger door as Becky jammed the keys into the ignition. A billboard-shaped cardboard cut-out dangled from the rearview mirror. GRAFFTI TEASE: WHAT DOES IT MEAN? The van stank from the overflowing ashtray.

"Where are we going?" Abigail asked.

"We, little sis, are going to bomb heaven."

"You in al-Qaeda or something?"

"Ha! You're funny. When I say heaven, m'dear, I mean the back of a freeway sign."

Abigail had no idea what Becky was talking about. She wondered again if Becky *wanted* to get her into trouble. Maybe then her father would send her back, cast her aside, leaving Becky alone once more to enjoy the life she cherished.

"Stop worrying!" Becky giggled. "Not *bomb* bomb."

BECKY JOHNSTONE WAS A confident, cocky driver. Abigail repeatedly checked her seatbelt as the van roared down the hills and then onto a freeway. She held the handle above the door for dear life, wondering if she could say "slow down" without sounding like a numpty. Bad form to change from Scottish punk to pathetic wimp in front of her new sister. Strange, she thought, if she'd met Becky back in Glasgow, she wouldn't have given the girl the time of day. Rich angst: what a load of self-absorbed bollocks.

With only one hand on the wheel and one eye on the road, Becky plugged in her iPod and swiveled her thumb. "Listen to this."

A news report blasted from the stereo: *"Vandalism around Los Angeles has exploded since the infamous Graffiti Tease campaign began. No corporation or sponsor has claimed credit. Addressing his party at a conference on crime in Washington last night, Lieutenant Governor of California, Dennis Howard, said that he intends to make the problem of teenage delinquency his first priority."*

The broadcast cut to a man's voice: *"It's not only about the graffiti. It's about the lack of accountability. Not long ago, the news was filled with positive stories about teens, about how they contributed—through communication, through social media, through the power of their voices. We heard how they raised awareness for their problems, how they pitched in for each other. We were inspired by kids who freed themselves from the shackles of their bad circumstances.*

"But where's the evidence? In vandalism? I'm not just looking at the graffiti. I'm looking at the data. Teen pregnancy has doubled in poorer urban communities. Drug and alcohol abuse remain rampant. Discussion of jobs, discussion of a future . . . There has been no progress. We've deluded ourselves into thinking we've made a difference. This newest wave of vandalism is ironically the best representation of what's happening to our most at-risk youth."

The presenter took over: *"Mr. Howard concluded with a promise to tackle the issue."*

The Lieutenant Governor came back: *"No more PC-dancing*

*around what needs to be done. We need to take firm action. And
we need to do it now. This is our future. Nothing is more important than our children.*"

Becky switched off the iPod. She reached over and plucked
a large pre-rolled joint out of the glove compartment, then
jabbed the car lighter. "That guy, the Lieutenant Governor,
that's who Dad and the Stepford are out with tonight. He was
speaking on the radio last week. What an ass." She withdrew
the lighter and sparked the joint.

Abigail wasn't sure what to say. For one thing, she didn't
really know why Becky wanted her to listen to it. And second,
the Lieutenant Governor didn't really sound like that much of
an ass. Abigail had come from a city that was rotting—thanks
in no small part to guys like Billy, who'd started their careers as
teens. If the guy on the broadcast was being sincere, if he really
thought that nothing was more important than children, then
great. Troubles should be dealt with.

She kept quiet, staring out the window as the van plunged
down off an exit ramp.

Very suddenly, after only a few stoplights, she saw that they
were in the depths of a rough area. Women stood on street
corners. Half the buildings were boarded up and covered with
spray paint. Windows were smashed. Shadowy figures stared
at their passing car. Abigail made sure the door was locked. At
least in Glasgow she'd learned to recognize, negotiate, and even
grade scariness. For example, the scary-rating for a group of
girls at a bus stop at 6 P.M. on a Monday: 0/10. Whereas three
staggering males in waterproof tracksuits in the city center on

Friday at 2 A.M.: 8/10. Now she found herself avoiding the eyes of a group of hooded teenagers loitering at the entrance to a 7-Eleven, drinking malt liquor. Garbage littered the parking lot. It was around 9 P.M. It was . . . hell, she couldn't even remember what day it was. Scary rating? She had no idea, and who knew what qualified as 10/10 in Becky's eyes?

Eventually, Becky stopped across the road from a large complex surrounded by a high razor fence. She yanked out her phone and thumbed a text message. A few moments later, she revved the engine. "Here they come."

Before Abigail knew what was happening, a boy in orange coveralls was scrambling over the fence. Another boy, dressed in street clothes—appearing seemingly from nowhere—grabbed the first boy and sprinted across the road. Together, they opened the back door of the van and jumped in. Becky drove off so fast that Abigail's head banged against the board behind her.

"Hey!" Abigail winced. "What's going on?"

Becky screeched left and Abigail bumped the left side of her head against the window. "It's okay. We're just taking Joe out for the night."

Abigail scowled, rubbing her temples. "Joe?"

"Stick's mate."

"Stick?"

"Stick's my friend. Joe's a kid he met one night out. He worked with us for a few months before getting caught. He's *our* friend. The boy's a genius."

"What are you talking about? Do you mind if I just go back to the house?"

"Can't. It's too late now. We won't be long."

Eventually, Becky stopped the van behind the huge grim pillars of a freeway overpass. "It'll be fine. Relax." She opened the curtain behind the front seat, revealing a small window on the back of the van. "Check it out."

Abigail knelt on her seat and peered through. The two boys were yanking the blankets aside, revealing buckets of glue, cardboard stencils, spray-paint cans, brushes of all shapes and sizes, and a ladder. Then they were opening the back doors and jumping out. The one in the orange overalls, Joe, must have been about fourteen; the other boy, Stick, a few years older.

"We're street artists," Becky said.

ARTISTS, MY ASS, ABIGAIL kept thinking. They were artists in the same way that Billy was an employment broker.

Their roles were clearly defined. Joe was the painter. On edge, with short-cropped hair and an angry scowl permanently plastered on an ashen, zit-marked face, he looked like any number of Glaswegian wannabe thugs. Not exactly "genius" material.

Stick was the minder and the photographer. Just as Billy might have been good-looking if poverty and crime hadn't throttled him, so too might Stick. Tall and slender, with puppy-dog eyes that were half-covered by a sideways fringe, his gene pool had equipped him with excellent raw materials. But he'd added a Graffiti Tease T-shirt two sizes too small, a pair of jeans two sizes too big, gaudy orange Adidas, and a baseball cap. Presto: handsome was now not-so-handsome.

Abigail stifled a sneer. She didn't come all this way to end up fancying guys like this. *Fancying guys like this.* The thought came out of nowhere. She was studying him too hard.

Becky had a role, too. She was the stencil maker and the transport.

And tonight, Abigail, the new girl, was the fittingly lame ladder-holder. A familiar role: she was being used.

She huffed as she grasped the bottom rung, perched at the foot of a large billboard—bare except for the words EXIT ¼ MILE. She'd never understood graffiti, why people would ruin things out of boredom. On the other hand, she knew all too well what bored people were capable of. The ladder wobbled precariously as Becky climbed to the top—stencils, bucket, and paint-roller in hand—and glued the cardboard cutouts to the sign.

When she came down, she said, "Good going, sis. Joe, up you go."

"Won't the drivers see us?" Abigail whispered.

"It's one of the risks, but Stick took care of the lights earlier."

Abigail glanced at the closest streetlamps. Only now did she notice that all within two hundred meters had been smashed. Despite the anxiety, she held the ladder firmly as Joe climbed up and painted inside the stencils, first with spray and then adding detail with the brushes. After a while, she recognized the creation as the one on the T-shirts she, Becky and Stick wore: five or more silhouettes of young people, all of whom had blank, featureless faces, some white, some black, and they were all dressed the same. They looked like zombies.

He seemed to take forever. Cars zoomed past. Someone beeped a horn.

Every now and then, Stick stopped to show her his photos of the work in progress. He never uttered a word, though she was acutely aware of his arm touching hers as he placed the phone in front of her. Gooseflesh rose as she stared at the images. A distant skyscraper loomed above the sign, silhouetted against a night sky tinted yellow with city lights and smog. She hadn't even noticed the building before. Backlit, the graffiti bounced from every picture, the zombies eerie and forbidding. Weird. The photos were somehow more powerful than the actual painting.

"Aye, nice," she finally mumbled. What else was she supposed to say?

The sound of a distant siren floated toward them.

"Quick, quick!" Becky shouted up the ladder to Joe. "Sign it!"

She threw materials in the back of the van as Joe dashed off a single large letter at the bottom: A.

"You got it all?" Becky asked Stick as Joe scrambled down the buckling ladder.

Stick nodded. "Got it. What do you think, Abigail?"

Abigail gritted her teeth, fighting to keep the ladder steady. The siren grew louder. Joe hopped over her arms to the pavement, and he and Stick tossed the ladder in the van.

"Get in!" the three of them shouted at her.

For a moment, she couldn't move. She stood, dumbstruck, at the bottom of the sign. She could not believe the situation she was in: standing at the side of an American highway, with a police car on its way. She had committed a crime. She was screwed. Her father might have pulled strings to get her a visa, but she wasn't a citizen yet. If she was arrested, there's no way he'd be able to stop them deporting her, surely. What an idiot she was.

"Come on!" Becky yelled.

Abigail jumped in the front seat of the van and slammed the door. Her fear turned to fury as soon as Becky screeched away, hurtling under the freeway and alongside roads at over 120 km an hour. But Abigail had to hand it to her: Becky was good at this, knew what to do, and where to go. She'd obviously fled the cops before.

The siren faded in the night.

IT WAS NEARLY 4 A.M. when the van lurched to a stop in front of the juvenile detention facility where they'd collected Joe and Stick. All was quiet. Nobody said a word as the back doors of the van flew open. Stick placed the ladder against the razor fence. Joe climbed up and jumped over it. But the moment Stick loaded the ladder back in and shut the doors behind him, an alarm sounded inside the grounds. Abigail stared in mute horror from the side mirror. Four uniformed men ran to Joe. He stood frozen as they tackled him.

"Damn it," Becky hissed, screeching off. "Shit. Poor kid."

Poor kid? Abigail almost spoke up. That's all Becky could muster, after they'd dumped him back in hell? But she bit her tongue. She didn't want to know how Becky truly felt at this moment. Anyway, the answer might sicken her.

⌒

HALF AN HOUR LATER, they parked out front of a ramshackle house in another run-down area. Once you were down from the hills, LA seemed to be an endless sprawl of flat slums. Stick jumped out the back and walked around to the driver's side window. Becky pressed the button to roll down the window

"The final letter," he gasped. If it was a triumph, whatever it meant, he sounded more resigned than pleased. "Joe did it."

"He did it," she agreed.

"So where are we at?" he asked breathlessly. His puppy-dog eyes flickered past Becky to Abigail. She stared down at her lap.

"Nearly ready," Becky said.

"When?" he pressed.

"Two, three days tops. We're running out of time. I think Dad's off the scent, but we need to be careful, you know?"

"Yeah," he said. "Mine's still sniffing around a bit. Don't think he knows though."

"Give me my phone. All the pics on here?"

Abigail shot them a quick glance out of the corner of her eye as Stick handed Becky the iPhone he'd used to take pictures.

"You sort the stuff in his den in case?" he asked.

"I did," she said. Her tone was grim.

"So, see you soon?" Stick leaned on the door, in no hurry to leave. He poked his head through the window, bringing his tired, sweaty face close to Becky's. "Sooner rather than later?"

Ah, right, Abigail thought. Stick was in love with her. Made sense.

"Off you go, sweetie. I'll let you know when." Becky kissed him on the cheek and pressed the button for the window to close. Stick jumped back. He frowned and chuckled, shaking his head. So: Becky didn't feel the same way. Despite her desire to ignore Stick, Abigail watched him in the side mirror as they drove off. He stood on the curb, staring back, until they were out of sight. *That was a very un-Billy thing to do*, she thought to herself.

THE SUN WAS THREATENING the east's black horizon when they parked the van in the driveway. After keying the alarm code and treading softly through the hall, Abigail noticed the grey backpack in the living room where she'd left it the day before—untouched by her father and Melanie. *Whew.* Grabbing it, she followed her sister up the stairs and into her new bedroom.

"Shut the door," Becky ordered, lighting a joint and flopping down on Abigail's bed. "Go on, have some. It'll help you sleep."

"I told you, I don't smoke." Abigail opened the window and tossed the backpack on the floor. She'd been hoping to unwind after the insanity of the evening with an actual conversation. But she realized that it was a stupid pipedream. Despite the luxury of their surroundings, this wasn't and would never be some Jane Austen story. She found herself imagining Miss Elizabeth Bennet painting graffiti on the walls of Mr. Darcy's mansion (*Darcy is a prick! Screw Darcy and his pride!*) then getting shit-faced and giggling with Miss Jane Bennet afterward. It didn't fit, and it wasn't right—not after what happened with that kid, Joe. And she didn't feel like showing Becky the letter or giving her the money. Maybe some other time. Right now, all she wanted was for Becky to get out of her room.

Becky exhaled a huge cloud of smoke. "You're angry."

Abigail waved it away from her face. "No, I'm tired. Anyway, what are you protesting against? Kidney-shaped swimming pools?"

Becky's smile widened. "Touché. What would a rich kid like me know about anything, right? But this, it's about everyone. All of us. Joe, too. Joe *especially*. More than you can imagine. You're worried about him, aren't you?"

Abigail swallowed. Funny. (Or the opposite of funny.) All she could think about was the scene in *The Shining,* when the little boy Danny asks the hotel chef if he's scared. The hotel chef lies, saying he isn't, even though both he and Danny know he's lying. They both know because the hotel chef has the "shining," too. So they both know that they're both terrified. All her life, Abigail had dreamed of a bond like this, hadn't she? And now that it was staring her in the face—not supernatural, but still undeniably bound, by *blood*—she was . . . what, exactly? Worried? Yes. But also grateful. Her sister knew exactly what was going on.

"You'll understand soon," Becky added.

"Stop with all the big mystery crap, okay? I don't care!" Abigail spat. "If we'd been caught, all that'd happen is they'd make you paint over your graffiti in an orange uniform. Me, I'd have been turfed back to Glasgow. And in case you're wondering, my life wasn't great there."

Becky's face softened. "I can only imagine. I'm sorry."

Abigail shrugged. She hadn't meant to play the sympathy card. But now she had, and her bottom lip was quivering.

"I didn't mean for you to be involved," Becky went on. "It was just bad timing. It had to be tonight. That's all I can say. And I care about Joe, more than . . . I care about him."

Abigail rolled her eyes. She got it. More mystery. She paused for a moment, then reached down and grabbed the joint from her sister's hand. After a long drag, she handed it back with an almost-smile. "Bollocks. Get outta here, okay? I need some sleep."

Becky managed a small laugh. She stood and touched her sister's face, gently placing her thumb on Abigail's still-quivering lip to steady it. "G'night, little sister."

CHAPTER SEVEN

"Morning, sunshine!" For the second time, Abigail woke to a strange voice.

"I have clothes! For you! And they're fantabulous!"

Abigail rubbed her eyes, squinting up at Melanie. "Hi. What time is it?"

Her stepmom was dressed in a white skirt and bright pink 50s-style halter top. "Nearly noon, sleepyhead!"

Abigail stretched and yawned. Melanie had placed a tray with orange juice, rye toast, and watery poached eggs on the table under the window. The snot-like eggs made Abigail gag a little. Plus, she hated rye bread. Perhaps she would ask Melanie for her favorite some other time: white toast with the wondrous and infamously "love-hate" black vegetable spread, Marmite. She suddenly panicked that she might not be able to get Marmite in the States. Then again, her father could "pull strings." He could probably arrange for a truckload.

"Voilá! This is for tonight." Melanie held up a bright red dress, very tiny, with only one strap. "What do you think?"

"Wow." Abigail wondered which tenth of her body the dress would cover. "It's . . . So, do you wear it over leggings?"

"Oh, just put it on." Melanie took Abigail's glass of orange juice and placed it on the table. "I want to see you."

Standing in front of the full length mirror moments later, Abigail wondered how to say it. *I look stupid. If I bend over, you will see the curry I had for dinner.* In the end she went for a blubbering: "It's, ah . . . wow. Um . . . I don't usually wear things like this."

"Well, that is a sin," said Melanie. "You could be a model, you know that? And *these* are the shoes, definitely!" She placed a pair of four-inch red heels at Abigail's feet. "On! On!"

There was no getting out of this. Abigail would have to wear the dress, and worse, she'd have to wear the shoes, even though they were so high they made her bum salute the ceiling. She'd read about the purpose of high heels in one of her "serious" library books—a text related to evolution. Apparently, heels were designed to make the female butt pout upward as if to say: *Here, here is my female monkey bit! Please bring on your male monkey bit so we will never be extinct. Save yourself. Save us monkeys. Wear the heels.*

Some of the other clothes were better, at least: jeans, T-shirts, trainers. The bikini was a little slinky. But the underwear was worse.

Melanie had guessed the correct bra size. Still, the sexy black embroidered lace-and-floral pattern were clearly not aimed at sixteen-year-olds. Abigail had no idea what Melanie was thinking. In honesty, she was a bit creeped out. *(Are you doing your bit for the monkeys, Abigail?*) As she touched the come-get-me lingerie, Abigail found her mind wandering in strange directions. Did Melanie want her to find a boyfriend? Did Becky have a boyfriend? (It clearly wasn't Stick, and Joe was too young; there was some deeper brotherly connection there.)

Abigail had never met a boy who'd tempted her back in Glasgow. She'd had offers, right enough. There was a sweet boy she kept bumping into at the Hillhead Library, for example. They chatted about Golding and Stephen Hawking a few times. Eventually, he'd asked her if she wanted "to go for a coffee." She'd said, "No, thanks." She switched to Mitchell Library after that. If their arms ever touched, she hadn't noticed. Her hairs definitely hadn't prickled. Library boy was nothing. He was blah. If he'd ever become something, he would have delved, asked questions, tried to make her need him. She didn't want any of that shite. She made a mental note to remember the mantra—*I don't want any of that shite*—in case she ever saw Stick again. It would probably be best if she didn't. Right. She had to snap back into robot mode. Robots needed nothing. No more late night "bombing" with Becky. It was settled. The see-through and lacy numbers would be for her eyes only.

At least she had clothes now. Most importantly, she had a swimsuit.

"Are there rules about the pool?" she finally asked.

Melanie laughed. "Yes. Don't drown in it." She rolled her eyes. "Of course not. This is your home. The pool is your pool. You hear me?" She placed her hands on Abigail's shoulders. "This is your home."

Abigail nodded. *My home.*

Melanie went on: She'd organized driving lessons (with Alberto, "who is wonderful!" starting next week). She'd bought Abigail a laptop and printer and had printed out information about the car service, local transport, shops, and her school, which would start in three weeks' time. And she'd made her an appointment to get her hair done.

"Oh actually, do you mind if I go somewhere else?" Abigail asked, retrieving the card Bren gave her from her backpack. "My friend is a hairdresser."

Melanie's eyes glazed over for a moment, as if the words didn't register. Then she smiled abruptly. "Of course! I'll drop you on the way to the caterers'."

Before heading downstairs, Abigail knocked on Becky's door. No answer. Without thinking, Abigail opened the door an inch, then regretted it and shut it again. She didn't have a clue how to be intimate with this girl. Hell, she didn't even know who Becky *was*, really. Only that wasn't true. Becky had shared something last night, hadn't she? But it was nothing Abigail could define. Passing concern for a kid in orange coveralls? No. It was more. It was crazy. Like the arm hair thing. A fuzzy thing that makes no sense and screws you up. Best ignored. Her mantra would be handy in relation to Becky *and* Stick.

I don't want any of that shite.

As she made her way through the sprawling house, she noticed that her father's den was closed again. She could hear a drawer banging shut, papers shuffling. She wondered if she'd ever even consider knocking on that door. But she already knew the answer to that one, too. *Probably not until I suss it out with Becky first.*

ABIGAIL WAS ASTOUNDED THAT Bren managed such a good job at the same time as talking non-stop.

He was a genius, it seemed. When she looked in the mirror she saw that he had maintained the essence of her personality—wary and tough—while adding never-before-seen elegance to her short, feathery blonde hair. In forty-five short minutes, he had given her the impossible: actual style.

Only twenty years old, and he was already co-owner of a salon in Beverly Hills. There must have been risks, Abigail imagined. But the squat premises were shiny and bustling and the phone rang constantly. Two movie stars were being worked on in the V.I.P. area. ("I could tell you who, but I'd have to smash your head against the Italian marble sink till you bled to death.") And everyone there seemed to love him, of course.

"When are you coming to my crib?" he asked. "None of this 'we must do lunch' crap. Before you go, we diarize." His house was on the Venice Canals, he told her. The back windows looked out onto the water, and there was a cute little bridge a few hundred feet away. "And I have a boat! A sleepover! How's a week from next Friday?" He wrote the date on a card, along with his home address and telephone number. "Bring booze and a toothbrush."

As she shambled back outside into the bright LA sunshine, trying to adjust to her new hair, she couldn't wipe the silly grin from her face.

Strange—she hardly knew Bren—but she knew she'd take him up on his offer. Another outsider, she supposed. But no, that sold him short; she'd known from the moment they'd parted at the airport that they were mates. There was no "shining." But there was no agenda, either. He cared. That was it. No weirdness at all like she felt with Becky. Or Melanie. Or Grahame. Or even Stick, for God's sake. Just comfortable. Watched out for.

LATER THAT NIGHT, GRAHAME, dressed in a kilt, caught Abigail hovering at Becky's door. "She'll be tapping away on that computer of hers," he said. "Leave her to it for now. Come join us."

When she was in the place called "care," the word "party" meant something awful and depressing. *Christmas party!* (Cheap tinsel, ten-year-old plastic tree, self-harming children ripping open thoughtless and impersonal cash-and-carry gifts). *Birthday party!* (Shop-bought cake for tearful abuse survivor). *Leaving party!* (Outdated disco music on cheap old-fashioned CD player that nobody would dance to. Why dance, when you knew you were leaving nowhere to go nowhere?)

But this party—for *her*, she kept having to remind herself—was a proper affair, one that *should* make a person feel happy. Over half of the grown-up men were dressed in kilts, all rented, no doubt, from the same extortionate and pretentious LA shop. Women attempted to outdo each other in dresses so glamorous they looked like a parody of some red-carpet movie premiere. Waiters carried trays of blue cocktails, "the same color as the

St. Andrew's flag!" (said Melanie, of course.) Waitresses served delicately presented vegetarian haggis and smoked salmon on oatcakes. Celtic music drifted through the garden and pool area. People smiled, talked, and laughed. There were only a few young people. The rest were friends, family, and colleagues of Grahame and Melanie's.

Abigail would never remember all the names. She wondered if she would ever, ever find anything to say to any of them. They were all aliens.

The chat was the same, over and over.

You look so like your father.

Sorry, what did you say?

What a change this must be.

I cannot understand that accent! Hilarious!

How wonderful that you finally found your family.

What? What are you saying?

Marlborough! You'll love it.

I didn't catch that. You sound just like Billy Connolly!

Do say something Scotch—let me hear the brogue…!

Exactly like Billy Connolly! You just have to laugh!

No one mentioned her mother. Either no one knew about her or she was a dirty word. In the whirl of being presented like an object, Abigail could once again slip back into robot mode. There must have been a reason her mother distrusted her father. But perhaps it was only resentment. While £50,000 was no small sum, this party alone probably cost half that. Maybe Sophie resented the fact that Grahame could have always taken care of Abigail without a second thought. If so, why the hell would Sophie have kept Abigail from him? Why the hell would she have left her to Nieve? And Abigail wasn't angry at Nieve; she *loved* Nieve. She loved Nieve more than she would ever love Sophie Thom. But was it that simple? Had her mother been as misguided as Becky and her friends? Was Abigail's fate all some part of some stupid protest against rich people?

Melanie, a tireless and gracious host, tugged Abigail this way and that and she played her part as best she could. It was surreal, perfect. Underneath, Abigail was only left with two desires: she wanted this to end, and she wanted to find Becky.

Then her father reappeared.

"This is Matthew," he said, tugging a lanky boy alongside him. "He and your sister are friends."

Abigail blinked. The guy was gorgeous, over six feet tall, with wavy dark hair that defied his Fudge hair product (she could smell it) and fell into his eyes—

Jesus Christ.

Matthew was Stick? Stick was Matthew? This guy?

Her pulse quickened. Her right hand was damp, she realized to her embarrassment, as she shook his. Those puppyish eyes flickered. He smiled politely.

She lowered her gaze. He wore smart trousers and a crisp shirt with a couple of buttons undone. She found herself staring at what she could see of his chest. Tanned. No hair. She shifted her gaze to the shoulders she'd not noticed the night before. Broad and straight. *Inappropriate.* She didn't know where the hell to look.

"Although Becky calls him Stick on account of his height," her father said.

"That's right," Matthew said evenly. He continued to stare back at Abigail as if she were a stranger, and released his hand. "I grew to this height at twelve. Used to be even more of a rake." His stare hardened, as if commanding: *Don't say anything, not a thing.*

"Nice to meet you," she croaked.

The words stuck. Time stopped. Everything in the room, everything but his eyes, faded.

"Well, you've certainly filled out now!" Grahame exclaimed, snapping her out of her trance. "And this is Matthew's father, my oldest and dearest friend, Mr. Howard."

Abigail forced herself to shake hands with a shorter, sterner, grown-up version of Stick. His father's hand was even clammier than hers.

"Friends since kindergarten, Dennis and me," Grahame said jovially. "Just like our kids. Dennis is the Lieutenant Governor of California."

"Oh! I heard you on the radio," she said automatically, mostly to distract herself from Stick. Bad move. How could she have heard him on the radio? She hadn't even been to the States when he'd been interviewed. And she couldn't explain what had really happened, that Becky had played the interview as Exhibit A of his evil ways.

Stick's father didn't seem to notice. He smiled with a politician's mock humility. "What did you think?"

"About unemployment and poverty? I thought you were

right. Something has to be done." Abigail's heart thudded in her chest. When she was this nervous, she knew it was always best just to stick to the truth.

"Smart girl," he said. "My son seems to disagree."

All eyes were on Stick now. He did a duck and dive: "I'm gonna go find Becky."

"I'll come with you!" Abigail knew she sounded over-enthusiastic. "Nice to meet you, Howard—I mean Mr. Howard."

Mr. Howard nodded. She followed Stick, but couldn't help glance back at the two men. They were already huddled in deep and serious conversation.

THE SHOES WERE A nightmare to walk in. Abigail wriggled each step, and felt ridiculous. How are legs supposed to do their job with a four-inch spike of red leather under each foot? *Shite*, that reminded her. The shoes were making her butt point upwards like a horny simian. She banished monkey-mating images from her mind and tried her best not to stare at the butt in front of her. It was difficult, though. The shape of him! Feck, now *she* was a man-monkey.

She focused on the carpeted stairs. She couldn't believe the gooey feeling. So yes, Stick was model-perfect and rich. But he was a vandal and in love with her sister. Annoyance with herself turned to anger at *him*. And now he was already ten paces ahead, halfway down the hall toward Becky's room. She would not be weakened by such stupidities. What did she care?

"Hey, wait!" she called. She stumbled, losing a shoe but still hobbling ahead.

He stopped and turned. "Yeah?"

"Why don't you leave Becky alone?" Abigail said. "You're going to get her into trouble."

Those eyes. For God's sake. Stick paused thoughtfully. "We're all in trouble," he said.

She sniffed. Well, no wonder he was in love with her. They were both riddle-ridden wankers. He knocked on the door, uninterested in further conversation.

Becky opened immediately. "Hey you two, how's the party? You getting to know each other?" She jerked her head toward Stick. "He cleans up all right, don't you think?"

"Apparently I lead you astray, Becky," Stick said.

"Aw. So you do . . ." Becky kissed Stick full on the mouth. "And I lead you." She slapped him gently on the cheek, but her touch made both sides of his face turn red.

Abigail's stomach churned. So, what *was* between these two? It angered her that her sister got to kiss those lips and she didn't. And it angered her that it angered her.

Becky had made a tiny effort to dress nicely, in silk trousers and a shoulder-less top. Even with the tiny effort, she was so much more beautiful than anyone at the party, certainly much prettier than Abigail. *There's no point in competing*, Abigail realized. She would never win. And why would she even want to, anyway? She *didn't* want to win. Win what?

"I'm sorry I threw you in the deep end last night," Becky said, ignoring Stick.

"It's okay," Abigail answered, still wondering about the kiss.

"It's not. But I won't do that again. Now let's go and do our family duty, shall we?"

Becky threw an arm over each of their shoulders and escorted them down the stairs. On the way, Stick leant down and picked up Abigail's missing shoe, passing it to her.

As if I'm Cinderella, she couldn't help but think. Too bad that was a lie, as well.

When they reached the garden, Grahame started to clink his glass with a spoon. Abigail asked a waiter if she could have a pineapple juice. The answer was no. He filled her glass with champagne instead. She'd never tasted champagne before. She sipped, keen to discover what all the fuss was about, and winced. *Yuck.* Stick veered off into the crowd. Becky led Abigail over to their father.

"As you all know, we're here to celebrate the arrival of my daughter," Grahame announced. His eyes were moist. His voice was thick. "Usually when you say that, the new arrival comes in a swaddling blanket and diapers. Well, as you can see, this one is potty trained."

The crowd burst out laughing.

Abigail's face flushed. Everyone, *everyone* in the room was now imagining her sitting on a potty. Some of them were imagining her in a nappy. A smaller amount had probably moved on from this image to consider her in her underwear. She looked down at her stupidly tiny dress. Perhaps they could *see* her underwear. Perhaps Stick could see it. She fidgeted with her bra strap, then touched her dress to make sure the line of her new lacy pants (now giving her the wedgie of the century) were within the boundaries of the red material. Stick was looking at her as she fidgeted. He probably had the nappy image in his head. A poo-filled nappy. *AGH!*

"I didn't know she existed till three days ago," Grahame continued. "As some of you know already, her mother was very unwell. I'm sad to say, she spent most of her adult life in institutions. She never told me about this wonderful gift . . ." He was tearing up.

Abigail smiled nervously. She'd never mastered crocodile tears, even in emergency situations like at US Immigration. She wouldn't be able to do it now, especially with all the underwear concerns bashing around in her screwed-up head. Becky must have noticed, because she grabbed the shaky hand at the bra strap and shoved it down between them, holding it tight.

"I don't know everything about her yet, but I know enough. Family is like that. I can tell that despite the difficulties she's had to endure, Abigail is a sensible, wonderful girl."

Sensible and wonderful. Not the adjectives Abigail would have used, but like he said, he didn't know everything about her.

A few people clapped.

"I feel so blessed that she's my daughter." He wiped his eyes.

Becky's hand fell away. Abigail almost shouted, *Becky's your daughter, too,* but bit her tongue.

"So, everyone raise your glasses to my daughter Abigail!"

"To Abigail!" everyone chanted in response, everyone but Becky.

"And here's lookin' up yer kilt!" Grahame Johnstone

attempted to joke in his best brogue. There were a few nervous laughs. He downed his champagne in one gulp.

Thank God. It was over. As the crowd applauded, Becky had already slipped away. Before Abigail could chase after her, Melanie appeared to continue parading her around.

ABIGAIL ANSWERED QUESTIONS AS best she could, repeating herself fifty percent of the time due to her stupid accent. But she could only concentrate on one thing: Stick and Becky, sitting close together on a bench in a dark corner of the garden. For the first time in her life, Abigail thought she might be going a little mad. She recalled late night parties at the camp on Holy Loch where the adults would get very drunk. There'd be toasts. Then guitars cracked out, then a heated political debate, then often an entertaining fight. Everyone would love *everyone*, except for a couple who would head out onto the main road to argue loudly. It would be hours before people went to bed.

Here, it was different. Eleven P.M., and the party was over. People had to drive home.

One hundred double-sided air-kisses later, the house was empty—except for Mr. Howard and Stick, who'd since vanished upstairs with Becky.

"Matthew!" Mr. Howard hollered from the door. "Time to go!"

Stick bounced down a few seconds later. He looked pleased, flushed, rumpled. Had he and Becky. . . ? *Who cares?*

"Thanks, Mr. Johnstone. And nice to meet you, Abigail."

Abigail extended her hand to shake Stick's. He leaned in for an air-kiss. She quickly corrected her mistake and withdrew her hand at the same time as *he* withdrew the air-kiss option and extended his hand.

He laughed. "Let's just nod at each other, cool?" His tone was dry, cheeky. "Great to see, er, meet you." Before he turned to follow his father out, he winked at her.

Mmm.

STOMACH STILL CHURNING, ABIGAIL watched as the hired staff whisked away leftovers and tidied the house. By midnight, she'd never have guessed there'd been a party at all.

"You did great," Grahame pronounced, as the last of them exited. "A proper little Johnstone. I'm so proud and happy."

Abigail found herself rubbing her eyes, too frazzled to question the compliment. She'd never been called a proper little anything before. "Thanks, Grahame . . . Dad. And you too, Melanie. It was lovely. Is there anything I can do?"

"You can get some sleep!" Melanie yawned—an actress yawn, with an exaggerated stretch to match. "That's what I'm going to do." She headed upstairs to the master bedroom.

Grahame was already heading to his den. "Night!" he called, closing the door him.

Abigail raced upstairs knocked on Becky's door.

"It's me!" she whispered. "Can you come to my room?"

"Okay," Becky's muffled voice replied. "Just give me a minute."

Abigail shut herself in her bedroom and opened her Nike backpack. Suddenly she was wide awake. She took out the grimy Mitchell Library books, placing them on the shelf in the corner. She dug past the plastic bag that contained her social work file: #50837. Finally, she removed the photograph of her mother, the letter, and the money, spreading them out on the bed.

Becky barged in wearing a bikini. "Midnight swim?"

"Sit down for a bit first." Abigail patted the mattress. "I need to show you some things."

Becky immediately zeroed in on the photograph. "Is that her?" She plucked it from the bed, almost reverently, and sat down beside Abigail, legs crossed.

"Aye. In Glasgow years ago."

Becky covered herself with the duvet. "Can hardly make her out," she whispered.

"I enlarged it. The only one I have, I'm afraid. Do you have any?"

"Are you kidding? He *erased* her. I always knew she existed, but she was off-limits. All he ever told me was that she was nuts. Said she heard voices and thought everyone was out to get her. Used to attack him and set fire to things. Hadn't brought her up in years until three days ago, when he told me about you. Even then, he said he didn't want to talk about that 'crazy woman.'"

Becky squinted to look more closely at the photo. "She's pretty, I think."

"She also left us some money," Abigail went on. "Twenty-five thousand pounds each."

"Wait. *What?*"

"You have twenty-five thousand pounds, care of our

mother." Abigail pushed the letter and the bundle of bills toward her sister.

Becky's eyes widened.

"And a letter. Do you want me to leave you alone while you read it?"

Her sister's forehead creased. She chewed a nail.

"Becky, I—"

"No, stay," she insisted. "I want you here when I read this. I wouldn't have known any of this if you hadn't shown up."

With trembling hands, Becky opened the envelope. Abigail hadn't reread her mother's letter since the day she received it, but she could almost remember it word for word. She tried to look at something other than Becky—the window, the bathroom, the walls—but couldn't help returning to her sister's eyes as they flitted from line to line. For a few seconds, Becky was expressionless. Then her lashes moistened. She was probably reading the part where her mother said she remembered her beautiful face.

Abigail hung her head, embarrassed.

Finally Becky let out a loud sigh. She folded the letter carefully. She chewed at her thumbnail again and whispered, "She knew."

"What do you mean? She knew Grahame was rich—" Abigail stopped mid-sentence, ashamed. *She* might be focused on the money, but why would Becky care?

Snapping out of it, Becky smiled. Her lips twitched. She struggled to slide the letter back in the envelope. She was anxious all of a sudden, and in a hurry. "No. Not that. I meant to say, I *wish* she knew. I wish she knew us. You and me."

Abigail nodded. "Are you okay?"

"I'm okay." Becky stood. A thousand thoughts were obviously whizzing around behind those frantic eyes. She grabbed the fuzzy photocopy. "Can I take this? Sorry, but I think I do need to be alone, after all."

Fair enough. Abigail nodded again.

As if in a trance, Becky took the money, the letter, and the photo and walked toward the bedroom door.

"When you're ready, I'm here," Abigail called softly after her. "Just knock."

But Becky was already gone.

CHAPTER EIGHT

Abigail hadn't slept well since Nieve had died. Survival depended on keeping one eye open in the beds she'd been forced to use since. Anyone could come in. Anything could happen. Not that she felt unsafe here. (No intruder, no matter how clever, could possibly bypass Grahame Johnstone's elaborate security system, with its buttons and codes at every point of entry.) But still she felt unsettled. Exhausted but not sleepy. To pass the hours as before, she tried to read.

The three books she'd brought from Glasgow annoyed her. *The Principles of Biochemistry*: too serious. *The Silence of the Lambs*: too dark. *Funny Physics*: not funny in the least. Anyway, she didn't feel like laughing. She could smell Glasgow in the pages, something old, oozing, and rotten. It was a smell she wanted to forget. She tossed the books under the bed beside the discarded Scottish prints and tiptoed out into the hall.

Becky's door was closed. The crack beneath was pitch black. No surprise. She'd have to wait until tomorrow to talk about the letter. Abigail made her way down the stairs into the living room. She switched on the soft library lights and crept inside, closing the door behind her. It was an old-fashioned place, packed with leather-bound books that did not smell of Glasgow. She touched the spines of some limited edition classics: Mark Twain, Robert Burns, Robert Frost, Walter Scott, Tolstoy, Dickens . . . She checked her fingertips with a secret smile. No dust.

The old vinyl seventy-eights in the corner were arranged neatly, their aged paper covers beautifully preserved. At first she'd been put off, but this was an okay hobby for a dad to have. Not quite cool, but nerdy and nice. She plucked one from the shelf and gazed at it. "Tonight I Am in Heaven." She put it back in and flicked through some others—then stopped. Her fingers landed on a song that Nieve used to play all the time: "Stormy Weather."

Before Abigail was even conscious of what she was doing, she took the record from the sleeve and set it on the gramophone. It had to be wound up, this machine, a proper antique. She rotated the gorgeous carved handle and placed the needle on the vinyl, cringing at the soft burst of noise. Was this even music? It sounded even worse than the stoned guitarists that used to sit around the commune campfire—fast one second and slow the next, never quite in tune, scratchy and awful. The version Nieve had played on her portable CD player wasn't as bad as this. Abigail remembered loving the song at the time, even the words:

> *Don't know why there's no sun up in the sky*
> *Stormy weather since my man and I ain't together*

Keeps raining all the time
Keeps raining all the time

Abigail imagined Nieve sitting at the small bench in the van, swaying as she listened. She flipped the record over. There was an inscription on the back of the paper sleeve.

To my darling Gray,
I miss you,
Forever, S x

Abigail squinted at the words. S could stand for Sophie. Was this a present from her mother to her father? She tried to picture it.

Grahame and Sophie, sitting on a couch. No.

Grahame and Sophie, dancing on a porch. No.

On the other hand, "S" had missed Grahame, if he was "Gray." They must have been apart a lot. *That* made sense. And if this was "their song," it was a bloody depressing one. That made sense, too. Their relationship had been doomed from the beginning.

Can't go on, ev'rything I had is gone
Stormy weather since my man and I ain't together
Keeps raining all the time
Keeps raining all the time

Abigail hurried back to her bedroom and shut the door.

SHE WOKE TO A man yelling. It was her dad, she realized. She threw on some clothes and hurried downstairs to see what the commotion was about. Becky was already a few steps ahead of her.

"What's wrong?" Abigail asked.

Becky shrugged.

"Come here now!" The voice boomed from the library. "Now!"

Abigail felt queasy as she walked in behind her sister. Her dad was standing beside the gramophone, "Stormy Weather" in hand.

"Who touched this?" he demanded. He was impeccably dressed in a dark suit, and looked nearly the same as he had last night. Yet his face was almost unrecognizable—his cheeks flushed, his eyes blazing, his jaw set.

She wanted to own up. But the words didn't come out.

"Do you know how valuable this is?" he snapped at Becky.

Abigail knew the accusation was aimed at both of them. Becky shot a quick glance at her. She could feel the blood draining from her face. She imagined that her skin now looked like the yellowed record sleeve.

"Well, do you? Tell me. Who's been handling my collection? Becky? Or Abigail? I understand you're new here, and perhaps where you grew up it's acceptable to fiddle with other people's precious things?"

Abigail swallowed, consumed with dread. It wouldn't be customs that would send her home. It would be her dad's rage.

Melanie appeared in an apron. "Honey, it's not damaged, is it?" she asked Grahame calmly. "There's nothing to be mad about, is there?"

Becky cleared her throat. "I'm sorry. It's my fault. A friend at the party last night wanted to hear what it sounded like."

Grahame's eyes bored into Becky. "A friend? You know no one touches these but me. No one! Especially this one." With hands shaking, he put the record back on its shelf; Abigail saw now that she'd shoved it back in the wrong spot. "No allowance for a month," he said to Becky, storming past them all.

Moments later, the door to his den slammed shut.

Melanie shook her head with an unreadable expression. Then she flashed an apologetic smile at Abigail. "Come and eat, girls. Your brunch will go cold."

It was an effort to force down the sickly eggs and hollandaise sauce. Abigail didn't just feel ill; she felt *babyish*. The little adopted baby who might ruin everything with her lies and misbehavior. After Melanie finally left, Abigail followed her sister's lead clearing the table.

"Thanks, for before," she muttered, her face hot. "I'll cover the allowance."

Becky shook her head. "Don't mention it. And no need for that."

Was their father prone to wild outbursts about his record collection? That would be handy information to have. But Becky seemed particularly distant. Maybe she was pissed off.

Or maybe she was stoned again. The two weren't mutually exclusive, Abigail supposed. Eventually, she gathered the courage to break the heavy silence: "What did you make of that letter then?"

Becky paused over the sink before answering. "I was wondering if we could just forget about it, for today. I want us to have some fun. Is that okay?"

It wasn't really okay, but Abigail nodded anyway. Fun wasn't her greatest skill at the most relaxed of times. Right now she was tenser than she'd ever been since Nieve had died. Her brain ticked over with information, trying to work out who was who, who liked whom, who hated whom, whom should she trust the least. But after Becky's rescue operation with the seventy-eight record, she was starting to think she might trust her new sister. As for everyone else, she had no idea.

Fun, though: what was that again?

"C'mon," Becky said, "let's go for a swim."

"I HAVE A CONFESSION," Abigail said, hovering at the edge of the pool.

"You're not really my sister?" Becky said, already submerged to her neck. She raised her eyebrows and smiled. "Sorry, bad joke."

"I'm not a very good swimmer."

"Don't worry. The pool is shallower than it looks. Jump in," Becky urged. "The water feels great."

If this was a dare, fine. Abigail flung herself into the air, hit the water and sank down, down, down. Panic flashed through her. Her feet finally touched the bottom and she sprung upward, breaking the surface with a sputter.

"You liar!" she gasped. All at once her arms were flailing about.

Becky was at her side in an instant, hauling her to pool's edge. "Shit, sorry, I thought you were joking. You really can't swim?"

"I really can't!" Abigail coughed water out and lifted herself out of the pool.

Becky stifled a guilty laugh. "I'm so sorry. How can you not swim?"

"How can you not be an idjit?" Abigail reached down and pinched her sister on her flawless bicep, quite hard.

"Ow! God, that'll bruise." Becky rubbed the red spot. But she was smiling again. Her glistening eyes met Abigail's. "Is this our first fight of the day?"

Abigail snorted. "If it is, you're getting off easy."

Eventually her breathing evened. Becky shoved a lilo across the water toward her, and she flopped into it, basking in the hard-hitting Californian sun. Becky's navel ring glittered: a flash of what looked like two very tiny silver birds, one on top of the other. Abigail wondered about her own belly. She was certain her skin would burn a lobster red, but she'd worry about that later.

"For the record, I wasn't trying to kill you or anything," Becky said slyly. "Not yet."

"I'm glad. If you had, you would've . . ." Abigail stopped mid-sentence. She was talking without thinking. She was about to reference Sophie. *You would've lost your sister, too.*

But Becky saw where she was going, anyway. "What was it like, seeing her dead?" she asked, climbing onto her own lilo and drifting beside her.

Abigail chewed her lip. "Well I can't compare it to seeing her alive. The worst thing is I didn't feel very much at all."

"Were you angry at her?"

"Yeah. I mean, my life was great till I was nine but, yeah, yeah, I was. Am."

"Me, too," Becky said with a sigh. "But I bet she had her reasons."

Abigail sat up. "What reasons could there be to abandon us and split us up? Did she ever try to look for you? Or me? I think she was just crazy, like your dad—*our* dad—said."

Becky closed her eyes and didn't answer. As far as Abigail was concerned, Sophie Thom was a mad selfish cow. End of story. Was there a different way of looking at things? Perhaps it was a bad idea to talk about it, for now anyway. She decided to change the subject.

"How come Stick's all street-kid one moment and all Hollywood-millionaire the next? I don't get him, or Joe. Or what you do. Any of it."

"Stick's like me," Becky said in a soft voice. "His father's a right-wing idiot. Mother's dead. His father made him major in Business Studies, so that's what he does during the week: study. He plays the role, like I do." She fumbled for her stylish bug-eye sunglasses, pulling them over her face. "We met Joe about six months ago when we were out painting. He used to do his stuff alone, but we got friendly and love his art. We think the same way. So he joined Stick and me. He didn't make it down the ladder in time a month back. We had to leave him. Now he's locked up. But that doesn't mean we don't give a shit. We'll get him out soon enough."

"So you three are the Graffiti Tease?"

Becky yanked off her shades and squinted at Abigail. "You catch on quick, sis. So has the press, just like Stick said they would." Her voice hardened. "Only they don't know who we are. You're the only other person who knows."

"I won't tell," Abigail blurted out.

She blushed, feeling childish, the way she did back on the commune when Nieve used to tell her to make up lies (namely, that she was Nieve's biological daughter) whenever the police came by, asking questions. But also privileged. Part of the conspiracy. Part of something bigger than her own meager existence. Part of the . . .

"Fun, remember?" Becky stated, unintentionally finishing Abigail's thought. "Today's about fun. I don't want to get all heavy right now. We've got all the time in the world for that. You and I have some serious catching up to do. Today is our fast-forward bonding day."

Abigail drew in a deep breath and smiled. "Deal." Here she was, on a lilo, in a swimming pool, with the most confusing but undeniably coolest person she'd met in a long time. Maybe ever. In spite of her curiosity, she found herself agreeing. What was the rush? "Heavy shit can take the low road." She kicked Becky's lilo, causing her to fall in with a splash.

—

"WHAT'S YOUR FAVORITE MOVIE of all time? I mean, if you had to pick one?"

By mid-afternoon it was practically thirty-five degrees, so Becky had hustled them inside, cranked the air conditioning, and made popcorn. She'd convinced Abigail to look through the huge collection of DVDs in the living room, promising that their father wouldn't get upset if any of them were misplaced. He had no interest in movies. Just old records. And his job, of course.

Abigail raised her index finger like a puppet and spoke in a squeaky voice, as if her finger were talking to her: an imitation of the telepathic little boy, Danny, from *The Shining*.

Squeaky-Voiced Finger: *"She wants to know my favorite film."*

Abigail: *"Don't tell her."*

Squeaky-Voiced Finger: *"But she wants to know."*

Abigail: *"Doesn't matter, don't tell her."*

"Shut up!" Becky spun around, eyes wide. "*The Shining* is totally in my top five favorite movies of all time. I'm serious! Dad knew that I wanted to see it, and after I complained a bunch, he let me, but watched it with me. He called it a horror movie. But it's so much more, y'know?"

Abigail paused for a moment before allowing her Squeaky-Voiced Finger to respond. *"Abigail, I told you never to tell anyone about our special film."*

Becky grabbed her iPhone and aimed it at Abigail. "Shh. Do that again. Let's make our own version. *The Shining*: Johnstone Sisters remake."

Abigail (smiling now): "*Worst. Idea. Ever. And now she's film-ing me.*"

Squeaky-Voiced Finger: "*Well stop her.*"

Becky giggled, squinting into the screen. "Stop distracting me. You're ruining the shot."

Abigail lunged for the iPhone. Becky ducked out of the way before donning a terrifying expression and lunging back with a: "HEEEERE'S BECKY!" Popcorn spilled all over the sofa. Abigail blinked at the mess. She laughed. She couldn't help it.

The Squeaky-Voiced Finger whispered: "*So this is what your sister is really like.*"

"OKAY, SO WE WON'T be Oscar-winning filmmakers," Becky muttered, attempting to watch the dizzy jumble after down-loading it to her laptop. She grabbed her car keys from her desk and dangled them in front of Abigail. "Next on the fast-forward bonding list: you're going to drive."

"I don't have my license."

"Well, Dad was able to save you from deportation, what makes you think he won't be able to save you from the traffic cops?" Becky pushed the keys to the van into Abigail's hand. "Don't worry, we won't drive on the street. Just out front."

Abigail sat quickly on Becky's bed. "Can't we just stay here?"

"Only if you get stoned." Becky flashed a wicked smile over her shoulder. "Kidding!" She snatched up the photo and letter Abigail had given her the night before. "Stash these back in your room. I made copies for myself." Before Abigail could protest, Becky was pushing her into the hall, shutting her door, and racing down the stairs, screaming: "Abi is a law breaker!"

Abi.

At first, Abigail tensed. But she felt nothing. No fight. No anger. No outrage. Nothing but the desire to run after her sister. She shoved the photo and letter in the backpack and followed her out to the van. Maybe Becky would always call her Abi. Becky and nobody else. Not their dad, whose temper frightened her. Not Melanie, who had no personality beyond trying to please everyone. If she allowed Becky to call her Abi, she might really have a sister.

THE WHEEL FELT OVERSIZED as Abigail gripped it, squirming in the cushion. She licked her lips. The heat was dry and suffocating. Becky shoved the key in the ignition for her and cranked the AC, talking Abigail through the controls slowly and carefully and showing her how to check the seat position, mirrors, and even the seatbelt.

Strange: Billy was the last person to have taught her something forbidden. "*What ya frettin' aboot, hen? Just light under the foil and breathe in through the tube. It's a lie one hit gets you hooked.*" She'd abandoned that lesson before it had even begun by slapping him in the face. Glasgow had never seemed further away. It was nighttime there, and probably raining.

"Breathe in for three while you're pressing down, out for three while you're releasing it," Becky coached. Within a half-hours' time, Abigail almost managed to relax. She stalled only once during her first circuit of the driveway. It wasn't that hard. It wasn't that much different from a video game.

"You're a natural, kid!" Becky exclaimed. "And look, you can press all these cool computer screens." She jabbed at a glowing button: SAT-NAV. "This is the most important. It shows your last destination, in case you ever get lost. But better let me take over now."

Abigail traded seats, and off they went. Becky turned off the AC and opened the windows, blasting some pop radio station. Soon they were tooling around Hollywood. The air felt cooler, the sun less oppressive than when Abigail had been driven from the airport. Hadn't Bren mentioned to her that nobody walks in Los Angeles? The streets were packed with tanned people in sunglasses, people who were beautiful, and people who tried their best to be beautiful. Even the shop windows seemed brighter and cleaner than she'd remembered on her drive in. "You want to see where the plastics live or where the real people live?" Becky asked.

Abigail was dying to see where the plastics lived, but was too self-conscious to admit it. "You choose."

Minutes later, Becky was parking at the ramshackle house where Stick/Matthew/Whoever had ended up the other night.

"What are we doing here?" Abigail gasped. "Stick's not a 'real' person?"

"Sometimes he is. Can you keep another secret?"

"Aye."

"We rented this place last month to stash all our stuff. I think Dad started suspecting I was up to something. Plus we needed room for the campaign, to make T-shirts and every-thing. But you can't ever tell anyone. Come in, take a look."

The house was even grubbier inside. There were no beds in the two bedrooms. Dirty coffee mugs littered the stained kitchen sink. The living room was an office-cum-studio-cum-storage space, full of stencils and paints, metal folding chairs, and a scuffed desk with a laptop, covered in papers. There were boxes of T-shirts on the floor and a badge-making machine.

"We usually come here at night," Becky said. "Will you help me with something?"

Back at the van, Abigail took a handle of the large rectan-gular box, covered by a thick blanket. Becky unlocked a small cupboard under the stairs in the hall and slid the chest inside. Abigail took a deep breath and dusted off her hands as Becky raced back to the van. When she returned, she had the file she'd brought from back home. She flipped on the laptop in the liv-ing room. "I want to show you something."

Abigail pulled up a folding chair and sat beside her.

Becky opened the file she'd brought in from the van. Inside was the photocopied photograph of her mother, the letter, and the money. She placed the photo beside the keyboard. Com-puter now fired up, Becky opened an attachment in her email and clicked onto a computerized image of Sophie at the protest march. "I scanned it and found some software to clarify. Look closely." She zoomed in on Sophie's face. It was much clearer than in the actual photograph. Becky had worked magic.

"God, she is beautiful," Abigail murmured.

"Yeah, but . . . not her. The guy, standing behind her, to her left."

"Oh, my God," Abigail whispered.

She remembered a scene at the very end of *The Shining*, where the director zooms in on a photo from the 1920s. It takes a while to recognize the main character, played by Jack Nicholson, because he's at least twenty years younger—fresh, happy, and dressed in completely different clothes. He's in an unfamiliar environment. It takes a while, but eventually you realize this is the same crazy middle-aged guy you've been watching all this time. Looking at this image gave Abigail the exact same creepy tingles. The man to the left of Sophie Thom was about nineteen years old and dressed in ripped jeans and a Ramones T-shirt. He had curly, shoulder-length brown hair. He was holding a NO NUKES placard. His mouth was open, yelling in protest. He was Grahame, her father.

"They were both in the Socialist Workers Party when they studied at Glasgow University," Becky said. "Just for a few months. But still. The freaking Socialist Workers Party. Ha! Can you believe it? I can't imagine the Navy would be too happy about that."

Abigail couldn't, either. She shook her head. Her father had been a radical? *And* a naval officer? Was that even possible? Something didn't quite add up. But that wasn't even the weirdest part, not for her at least. No, it was that he and her mother were both students at the university she'd walked past so often, filled with anger and envy—the place she'd so desperately wanted to be part of and never could be. She was a *legacy* there.

"He was there on some sort of program with the armed forces," Becky added. "He came back here after graduating and joined up with the Navy full-time for a few years."

"That must be when she sent him that record, 'Stormy Weather,'" Abigail said, unable to tear her eyes from the computer screen. "She wrote on the sleeve that she missed him."

"I found these in the attic too . . ." Becky opened a box under her desk. Inside were tapes and CDs. "He made her a mixed tape every year from nineteen eighty-nine, when they met, onwards."

Abigail picked up the first tape. *To my darling Sophie, nineteen eighty-nine*, was written on the front. The tracks were listed neatly on the case. All of them love songs. There were tapes for 1990, 1991, 1992, 1993, 1994. All titles of a weak-kneed, smitten romantic. She recognized some of them: "Nothing Compares To You," "How Am I Supposed To Live Without You," "Opposites Attract," "From A Distance" . . . "I Will Always Love You." Some, she'd never heard of before: "Price of Love," "I'll Be There," "Don't Let the Sun Go Down On Me," "Have I Told You Lately," "Stay."

"So they were really in love," Abigail said, half to herself.

"Looks like it. But I don't think they could make the long-distance thing work. Anyway, when he came back he must have changed. I know he got even closer to Dennis Howard." She smirked. "Guess he traded in the Ramones for his seventy-eights and Marx for Fox News."

Abigail blinked. Becky had lost her. "But they still got back together? Mum and Dad?"

"Yeah, he went back to Scotland, to serve at some submarine base. They were together there from nineteen ninety-two to nineteen ninety-six, till I was born and she started losing it, so the story goes. But, Abi, you're missing the point. Check out the mixes. He didn't stop."

Abigail leaned over and flipped through the jewel cases in the box. There were more CDs: one a year, right up to 2012. Cheesy mush like "My Heart Will Go On" and "You're Beautiful" and "Angel."

"My God, he loved her all that time."

"I think he still does," Becky said.

"But she was mad. Wasn't she? I don't get it." For a moment, Abigail almost felt sorry for Melanie. The poor woman probably had no clue.

Becky zoomed in again so the two faces took up the screen. "Funny how two people start off the same then wind up being completely different," she said.

"Kind of like us," Abigail said. She immediately regretted the words. She wasn't even sure why she'd said them. But she wasn't thinking of Becky. She was thinking of that woman in the photo, wondering how any mother could possibly hold two infants in her arms—two in a row—and then abandon them both.

Becky just chuckled. She placed the tapes, CDs, the photo, and the file back in the box and switched off her computer. "We're the same. You just don't realize it yet." She picked up the box and put it next to the large rectangular chest in the cupboard under the stairs, then shut the cupboard door and locked it.

Maybe it was best to steer clear of family heaviness. Today was supposed to be about fun. On the other hand, what else was there? It wasn't like they had friends in common, was it? But even as she asked herself the questions, she knew the answer. There *was* something between them. Back in the van Abigail decided to ask something she had begged herself not to ask. Saying the words would mean that she cared. Then again, she supposed she did.

"Is he your boyfriend? You know . . ."

"Stick! Shit, no. Not that he hasn't tried." Becky fidgeted with the steering wheel, as if she couldn't decide whether to go on. In the end, she shrugged and smiled, turning to give Abigail the stare she was growing used to. "Let's just say I'm not interested in sticks."

Abigail blinked. She nodded. She didn't want to appear shocked, or overly impressed, but she was both. Score another one for Becky. This girl, this person, this *sister*, was a bottomless well of surprises. Plus, there was the bonus: she wasn't Stick's girlfriend.

And never would be, Squeaky-Voiced Finger finished in silence.

CHAPTER NINE

The guard's growl was a familiar one. "You can't take that in here!" Give the guard a brogue, he'd fit right in at a detention center in Glasgow.

"Right you are." Becky handed over her iPhone and took a seat in the visiting area, gesturing for Abigail to join her.

The room was also depressingly similar. Leaflets littered the dirty walls: DRUGS HELPLINE! SUICIDE HELPLINE! USE CONDOMS! DO YOU KNOW ABOUT HEPATITIS C? ALL YOU NEED TO KNOW ABOUT IMMUNIZATIONS! She wished they could be back at the house, splashing each other in the pool.

Instead, Becky had brought her to a place filled with Unloved Nobodies. It was their last stop before heading home to drink cocktails and "get a swerve on." Abigail had also made a mental note to divert Becky from the getting-a-swerve-on idea. They could go for another swim, or watch a movie . . . or something. She'd at least *try* to keep Becky from writing herself off every day. Becky obviously gravitated toward people less fortunate than herself. Becky wanted to help. Abigail got it; *she'd* wanted to help Camelia. But Abigail hadn't had a choice. Why did Becky need to immerse herself in the lives of the miserable? Who would *choose* to do this?

"Hey!" Joe called, shambling through a door. He flopped in a plastic chair beside them. His orange coveralls seemed filthier and baggier. He was skinnier, more pimply. Dark circles ringed his eyes. "How's it going? You okay? Me, I've been better." He fumbled for a pack of cigarettes. "*Assholes!*" he barked for the benefit of the staff. "The assholes gave me solitary. And I'm expecting three extra months at least." He struck a match.

"Hey! No smoking, Dixon."

Joe eyeballed the guard as he took a long puff and exhaled.

A stand-off. Abigail swallowed. The guard strode over and snatched the butt from Joe's mouth, grinding it out on the floor with his boot. Neither he nor Joe blinked. The guard returned to his station. Life resumed.

"Have you been working today?" Becky asked.

"Nah, they took away my paints and brushes." He was fidgety, Joe. Constantly bouncing around in his seat, radiating energy and discontent. Abigail didn't want to offend Becky, and she *was* concerned, but a part of her wanted to get as far away from him as she could. She felt grubbied, as if she were back at the Solid Bar with Billy.

"Can you get them back?"

Joe sneered. "These ASSHOLES can keep them forever if they want."

"Oh, well." Becky chewed her lip. "That sucks."

He finally sat still. "We're getting our shots tomorrow."

"Shots?" Abigail asked.

Joe pointed at the immunization leaflet with a frown. "MMR: Measles, Mumps, Rubella."

Becky stiffened, sitting upright. "What—What time?" she stammered.

"Afternoon."

Abigail peered at her sister. Becky had turned noticeably pale, as if her tan were painted on top of dead white skin. Ah, well. Abigail could relate. She hated needles, too. She and Becky really *were* connected. Sort of weird that Joe was getting the triple whammy now, though. The MMR was usually administered during infancy—or in later life if the recipient had HIV—or so she'd learned from a smelly text on a night alone at a Glasgow library not long ago. But . . . maybe he'd been severely neglected? Or was HIV positive? The thoughts hadn't occurred to her until now. She knew nothing about Joe. Not even his last name.

Becky did, though.

Abigail squirmed in her plastic chair, suddenly guilty about wanting to run home to the sunny pool and the popcorn and giggling. "Have you ever had an MMR before?" she asked him. "It's probably not that bad."

"No, I know I got it when I was a baby. They said it's a booster—" Before Joe could finish, there was a burst of swearing and shouting through the window.

Abigail turned and stared into an open-air quadrangle. Four teenagers were in the midst of a brawl. One had a knife. Alarms sounded. Staff raced to the scene, keys jangling. They were too late, it seemed. One of the youths was down, bleeding. The others had fled the scene, only to be wrestled to the ground by a gang of burly guards—a repeat of what she'd seen happen to Joe.

"Fifth fight today," he said, without emotion. "Same old, same old."

Becky was visibly trembling, however. Not that Abigail could blame her. The truth of the matter was that Abigail was probably a lot more like Joe than Becky in certain ways. A knife fight was no big deal.

"You okay?" Abigail asked.

"Fine," Becky said, avoiding her and Joe's eyes. She forced a deep breath. "I'll come back in the morning, get you out somehow. In the meantime, try and chill out."

Joe flashed a mirthless smile. "I'll keep doing what I've been doing. Nothing."

"All work and no play makes Joe a dull boy," Abigail joked lamely, referencing *The Shining*.

The joke fell flat. Becky's expression remained distant, as if she hadn't heard.

A fleeting smile crossed Joe's lips. He tilted his head at Abigail. "Well, you've had your whole fucking life to think things over. What's a few more minutes gonna do you now?"

Abigail nearly laughed; it was a line from *The Shining*.

Joe took hold of Becky's hand, serious again. "Listen, Becky, whatever happens, don't ever feel guilty. It was worth it. All of it. The buzz. The work, it's kept me going, y'know?"

Becky nodded, snapping back to the moment. "I know."

She looked him in the eye. "I love you, Joe, you know that? You still got that cellphone hidden?"

"Yeah."

"I'll text you later. We'll find a way to get you out of here first thing in the morning." She kissed him on the forehead. "In the meantime, hang tough."

A tear fell from Becky's cheek.

Abigail's breath came fast. She stared and turned away. It was the first time she'd ever seen her sister cry. As Joe was being escorted back into his prison (shaking off the guard's arm, calling him an ass and a dick), Becky whispered to herself, "Tomorrow afternoon . . ."

ON THE DRIVE HOME, Becky was sullen, inscrutable. She stared straight ahead without talking. Abigail picked up Becky's blank iPhone, mostly to see what her sister kept as a wallpaper. Not surprisingly, it was a "B," scrawled in graffiti.

"It's nine-seven-four-six," said Becky.

"What?"

"The pin to my phone. Nine-seven-four-six."

"Oh, that wasn't why I was looking. I don't need—"

"Just in case you do, one day. I hide it in my hiking boots."

INSTEAD OF "GETTING A SWERVE ON" together as planned, Becky went straight to her room and shut herself inside. Abigail wasn't sure what to do. She didn't want to get pissed, but no doubt Becky was probably getting high alone in there. Besides, Abigail didn't want the bonding to end. Did it have to? She paced around her room for a while and then knocked on her sister's door, keen to be assertive. Something had freaked Becky out back at Juvie. Abigail wanted to know what. She also wanted to thank her for the day—for all of it, for trusting Abigail and including in her life without any questions or resentment.

Right: start with a thanks and a hug. If Becky was getting stoned or turned down the gesture, fine. Abigail could handle the embarrassment. Better to be honest about how she felt.

Becky opened a few seconds after Abigail knocked, two pink, fizzy cocktails in hand. "Hey, do you remember if I turned the computers off before we went out?" she asked. The color had returned to her face. She was smiling crookedly. She jerked a shoulder toward her monitor.

Abigail swallowed. The stink of alcohol made her wince slightly. "Um . . . They were off when we were here last, I think."

"Shit, really?"

"Why?"

"They're on now. I don't remember switching them back on. Oh, I probably did when I came in without thinking about it. I'm getting paranoid. Chin-chin!" Becky handed Abigail one of the martini glasses. Pink liquid sloshed over the side as she clinked. She took a big gulp then set her glass down and began rolling a joint.

Well, so much for the speech and the hug. So much for diverting Becky from getting wasted. She wouldn't even make eye contact. "Are you okay?" Abigail murmured.

Becky licked the rolling paper and sighed softly. "I'm sorry, but I am really, really busy tonight. Can we take a rain check? Will you be all right if I get on with it?"

"Sure." A rock landed at the bottom of Abigail's tummy. "But please tell me, is everything all right? You're upset, since visiting Joe."

Becky lit the joint and took a drag. "Well, it's a sad place." Her hand was shaking. "Why don't you take your drink with you?" She pointed to the blender on the desk, three-quarters full of what looked like pink slime.

"I'm not thirsty," Abigail said.

Joint in mouth, Becky had turned around and started tapping away at the computer. She wasn't even listening anymore. Was she on some kind of website or blog? All Abigail could make out was two lines: *THE TEASE IS OVER! So only the rich need fire in their bellies?*

"Becky?"

"If you don't want a drink, I left some candy in a dish. Saltwater taffy." Her sister didn't as much as blink.

Abigail returned to her room. After slamming the door, she poured her margarita down the sink, pulled *Funny Physics* out from under the bed, sniffed it, and threw it on the floor. There was no bowl of candy in her room, either. Big surprise, that.

CHAPTER TEN

"Abigail. Abigail, darling."

Abigail opened her eyes to find her father sitting beside her on the bed. An alarm went off in her brain. *Something's wrong.* Grahame had called her darling. His eyes were bloodshot. He had his hand on her arm. It was shaking.

"What is it?" Abigail sat up. She glimpsed Melanie standing at the door, her eyes also moist and red. The curtains were half open. The sun was quite high in the sky.

"Something . . . terrible . . ." Grahame choked on the words. He blew his nose on a large tartan handkerchief.

Her heart started thumping. "Tell me."

"Becky."

Without waiting for more, Abigail jumped out of bed and ran across the hall. The bedroom door was open. Two police officers—one male, one female—were hunched over something next to the bed. Abigail pushed her way in between them.

Her breath caught. That something was Becky: lying on the floor, dried white froth at the corners of her mouth, vomit on the carpet, eyes open. Abigail's knees seemed to give out. She crumpled beside her sister. "No. No, no." She lifted Becky by the shoulders and held her, rocking. The flesh was cold. This made no sense. Becky was fine when she'd last seen her. She'd been typing and drinking and smoking—

"I'm sorry, miss, but you have to stop that," the female cop interrupted. "You can't touch anything. I'm sorry."

Abigail couldn't let go. Last night she'd wanted to hug her. She should have. *Rewind, rewind,* Abigail thought desperately. *It is last night. Becky's hugging me back. Her arms are around me and she doesn't want to get rid of me and she doesn't want to get me into trouble and she loves me and she's warm and I'm warm inside and I'm smiling—*

"I'm sorry," the officer repeated.

There would be no rewinding.

Abigail gently lowered the cold body to the ground. She'd seen violence. She'd seen tragedy. Fights, abuse, blood, teeth knocked out, even stabbings. But this was *death*, only the second corpse she'd seen in her life. Two corpses in a week. One, her mother; the other, her sister. Both strangers. Both the opposite of strangers. She kissed Becky's clammy forehead. It didn't feel like skin. She didn't know what it felt like. Reflexively, she wiped her lips.

Jesus. Her throat tightened. Her eyes began to sting.

"Miss, you really must leave," said the male police officer.

"Just . . . one second," she choked out. "Please."

Neither officer argued. Perhaps they could see into her brain, perhaps they could see that she regretted not taking more time with her mother. Perhaps everyone in America had the shining. Whatever the reason, the police-officer couple allowed her to sit over her sister for just a little while, taking in her dark lashes and her perfect little nose, now unfortunately smeared with white powder. Abigail's blurry eyes roved over Becky's square shoulders, the high insteps of her feet, her skinny forearms, and slender, toned, tanned legs. She stared and stared, burning every detail into her memory. Lovely, troubled Becky . . .

"That's enough now," the male cop finally said, helping her to her feet.

"I want one last look at her room. I promise not to touch anything."

She shook free from his grasp. She knew exactly why she wanted to do this: the video they'd shot would not wind up confiscated by the police. She poked her head in the bathroom and then darted into the walk-in closet. There were the boots, tucked behind a pair of trainers. Before he could catch up to her, she dug in the left boot—*not there*—dug in the right, and her fingers clasped around the iPhone. *Thank God for small favors,* she thought. Her throat tightened. She wiped the image of Nieve from her mind and shoved the phone into her bra just as he appeared behind her.

"What are you doing?" he snapped.

"Just looking to see . . . if she left a note," Abigail said feebly.

It wasn't a lie; she really wanted to know. She brushed past him into the room. There were traces of white powder on the desk. Becky had said she'd only smoked pot. Maybe she was too ashamed to admit a more serious drug problem. By the looks of it, Becky had guzzled almost a liter of very strong margaritas (the blender was empty) and a bottle of red wine (upside down in the bathroom sink); plus she'd smoked two joints (snuffed down into the china saucer-turned-ashtray by the window) . . . a bag of powerful-smelling marijuana lay open on the bed. Saddest of all, two empty pill bottles lay open next to her right hand.

"No note that we can find," the female officer said.

As Abigail backed out into the hallway, dizzy with shock, a thought struck her. The room was a mess as far as the booze and drugs went. Yet Becky had tidied up everything related to her other secret pastime. Her stencils and paints and brushes were gone. The paperwork once strewn all over the desks and floor was gone, too. Maybe she'd snuck out in the middle of the night and taken it to that weird house, the "Headquarters" she and Stick rented.

All of a sudden, Abigail noticed that Becky's computers were gone, too.

Had the police already taken them for some reason? How could someone so chaotic and drug-addled be so organized at the same time? Wouldn't someone so organized have written a note? What the hell was Becky's problem, anyway?

Why did you do this, you idiot? Abigail felt like screaming.

Black dots swam at the corner of her eyes. Her head spun.

At that moment, a pair of arms wrapped themselves around her waist. It was her father.

If he hadn't caught her, she'd have fallen unconscious to the floor.

CHAPTER ELEVEN

Lying on her bed, staring at the ceiling, Abigail wondered if she were a phony. The black hole at the center of her belly couldn't be real.

She hardly knew Becky. She hadn't warmed to Becky to start with, and probably would have never understood her politics or her Graffiti Tease "art" or her mood swings. Abigail could sort only through the facts, the evidence. All amounted to the same: Abigail Thom ruined everything. Wherever she went, disaster struck. She should never have come to LA.

Three days—three measly little days in her presence—and an innocent eighteen-year-old girl had died. So that initial fear was probably spot-on: Becky must have been overwhelmed by her new sister. Jealous, even. Shoved out of the way at the party, by her father's speech, the whole circus. Abigail had driven Becky over the edge. Was that why she was hurting?

Her mother's death hadn't had much impact. Then again, Mum was a dream; Becky was a promise. The promise of family and of friendship. (For fuck's sake, for the first time ever,

Abigail had reveled in being called "Abi.") Now that promise lay motionless on the floor of an LA bedroom. Becky was
dead, ugly-dead: froth, powder, booze, pills, vomit. Abigail
had learned dead was never pretty, and now she'd learned dead
could never promise anything but an end.

Without the painkillers, Becky's autopsy might read "Death
by misadventure." That's what the authorities called ODs in
Glasgow. More euphemisms, supplied by idiots in charge. Misadventure: such a playful word. Death by Playfulness. Death
by Idiotic Horrible Accident, more like. A bottle of pills wasn't
a fun night gone wrong. It was suicide.

Abigail wiped her eyes on the duvet, clutching Becky's
iPhone to her chest.

At least Melanie and Grahame had left her alone. Of course
they had. They weren't Nieve; they weren't even Arthur at No
Life. They didn't know her, so they couldn't console her. Nor
she, them.

Hours passed. Abigail could hear people talking in the
room across the hall. She could hear doors opening and closing, the body being taken away, cars coming and going in the
driveway. She covered her head with a pillow, squeezing down
on her ears. She did not want to hear.

Don't come near me, she willed. *Don't anyone come anywhere
near me.*

But it was self-pity rather than grief. She knew that now.
Weakness, she thought again and again as the sun turned her
shades a fiery orange and disappeared.

Poor, poor Abigail. A happy future: gone. A good life: splat.

Well, screw weakness. Screw it all. She wondered if she should just get back on the plane, go back to Glasgow. At least there she knew how to deal with unhappiness, having never expected anything else. Here, in this weird wonderland-now-hell, she had no idea how to cope.

TWO DAYS LATER—AFTER silent meals, after silent retreats into silent rooms, and after the very occasional silent hug (Abigail counted three with Melanie, two with Grahame: all random)—she sat with her new parents in the backseat of an old-fashioned, shiny-black car. It was like the ones Royals took to do that dumb wave, minus the pageantry.

A long line of similar vehicles followed them. Down they went, through tree-lined streets . . . past the gated houses, out of the neighborhood, and finally along the beach. The hearse led the way, Becky in charge of this somber parade.

Grahame sobbed occasionally into Melanie's shoulder. She wiped his tears with her hanky, held him tight.

Abigail had cried however long she'd needed to cry in private. Right now, she held in her tears. She observed. There was no way in hell she'd ever go back to Scotland. Of that she was sure. She wasn't exactly in robot mode. She wasn't sure if she could ever return to robot mode again. But she refused to break down.

Besides, she was a pro at death. This was the second funeral she'd attended in a week. Of course, only three people had managed to make her mother's: four if she included the priest.

Her sister's funeral was the polar opposite. The church was overflowing with well-dressed mourners, choir singers, violinists, and extravagant floral arrangements.

As Abigail took her seat in the front pew, her eyes zeroed in on the large portrait of Becky. There she was, pictured on a sumptuous, rose-littered table near the coffin. Interesting: that smiling face in the photo was quite a few years younger than the Becky she knew. Long hair. Fresh-faced. No piercings. Grahame had obviously chosen a shot that he approved of.

As for their father, he'd written a eulogy, but only managed a few words before collapsing into a blubbering heap. Mr. Howard walked up to the front of the church and rescued him, taking the sheet of paper and reading out the story of Becky's life. Amazing, like a true politician, he managed to make the speech sound fact-ridden and insincere. "*She loved art at school, was an excellent swimmer, made an impression on everyone she met . . .*" If Becky could hear, wherever she was, she'd be rolling her eyes and exhaling big puff of pot smoke.

As for Melanie, who knew what was going on under that black hat? Maybe Melanie was a bit glad. She was so very still in her tight black dress, meticulous makeup, and perfect hairdo. Maybe she worried that the slightest movement would betray the truth: *I am free.* The difficult teenage step-daughter was gone; replaced by a pliable new one, grateful to have been saved.

Abigail began to feel sick. She snuck a quick scan of the congregation, hoping to spot Stick. She wondered which costume he'd choose to wear, graffiti artist or posh ass. He was the only person she wanted to talk to, the only person whose shoulder she would have welcomed.

He wasn't there.

The last time Becky had seen him, she'd called him "sweetie."

Not so sweet after all, Abigail thought numbly. Maybe that was for the best.

THE CEMETERY WAS PERCHED on a bluff overlooking the ocean. A very expensive plot, by the looks of it, with room for the rest of them when it was their turn.

How tidy! Abigail thought as the coffin was lowered into its hole. *This is how it all ends. I will be buried in a place I don't know with a bunch of people I don't know.*

At the graveside, a girl Abigail's age read a pretentious poem. (The girl hadn't been at Abigail's homecoming party.) Another stranger sang a tear-jerking ballad. Abigail had only known Becky for a few days, but she knew Becky would have howled in protest at this charade. She found herself thinking of Nieve's funeral. She knew nothing about it, but she was at least certain it had been *real.* She knew it had been down-to-earth, honest, appropriate. It hadn't made Nieve out to be a saint, hadn't overly celebrated some random part of her life. (Swimming competition? Really?) It had been the kind of funeral that would have been perfect for Becky.

Oh, how tasteful the hors d'oeuvres at the reception afterward!

How plentiful the excellent wine!

How sad, sad, sad all the strangers!

That wasn't entirely fair. Grahame's suffering was real. He sat quietly at the bar, drink in hand. Mr. Howard and Melanie took turns to comfort him. Abigail felt too awkward to make her own move. Besides, what could she say? A hug might prompt some outburst, and she didn't want to start crying, not here. So she kept her distance. But mostly she was afraid. She was afraid of what he *really* thought, what everyone really thought.

Three days after Abigail had snatched a spot in this family, Becky had snuffed herself out.

Whenever Abigail caught someone's eye, she couldn't help but wonder if they were rendering judgment. *You're no better than a murderer.*

Enough. Time to leave. She strode out the door, down the driveway to a steep rocky path that led to the shoreline, and past boats moored in front of an exclusive yacht club. Soon, she was onto the beach. Kicking off the heels Melanie had bought, she walked barefoot in the hot sand for a long while—further and further away, as far as possible from that tragic farce of a funeral reception. *For Becky!* Exhausted, she sank cross-legged in the shade of a secluded dune. No use caring about ruining her new dress; she'd never wear it again. She wiped the sweat from her brow and touched the chain and key around her neck, the one Nieve had given her. It was a small, insignificant object, like her mother's photo. Like Becky's iPhone. Artifacts of the dead.

Almost without thinking, Abigail pulled the iPhone from the black Hermes purse Melanie had loaned her. In the past forty-eight hours, she'd keyed the pin number a few times, 9746—and had even found their *Shining* video file—but she hadn't mustered the courage to open it. Now, sitting in the sand all alone, Abigail pressed PLAY.

Waves crashed on the shore in front of her as the small screen lit up. An unpleasant thought occurred to her as she stared at the tiny, jerky image of herself. Did Becky already know what she was going to do? Is that why she'd suggested they focus on fun that day? Is that why she'd made a point to tell Abigail both the pin number and her phone's hiding place?

Abigail: "She's filming me."

Squeaky-Voiced Finger: "Well stop her."

Abigail: "I don't know how."

Squeaky-Voiced Finger: "Grab it, grab it, the phone, grab it."

Becky's face filled the screen. "HEEEERE'S BECKY!" Popcorn. Laughter. The image spun abruptly from floor to ceiling.

Abigail thought that the video might bring her to tears. But now she was confused and pissed. The girl who'd made this silly little film was raucous, full of life. And that night, she'd killed herself? Abigail watched the video again, pausing on the close-up of her sister to study her face: bright, intensely happy, almost unbearably beautiful. She replayed. Then again.

With each viewing, Abigail's confusion intensified. She remembered something Becky had said in the pool: *"I don't want to get all heavy right now. We've got all the time in the world for that."* She remembered how the visit to Joe at Juvie had affected her, how she had promised to break him out the following day. Something had upset her when they were with him, something she'd wanted to hide . . .

Abigail's grip on the phone tightened.

Back at the house, Becky had mentioned that her computers were back on. It was one of the very last things she'd ever said, in fact. If she *had* killed herself, something must have happened to drive her to it. Had somebody wanted her to see something? Had someone been snooping around and discovered something they shouldn't have? Was that why the computers had been confiscated?

Shite. Abigail might have been clutching at straws, anything to believe that her sister was not consumed by depression and hopelessness—anything to ease the guilt that Abigail's arrival had contributed to her death. But, no: it didn't add up. Becky wasn't that good an actress. *Nobody* was that good an actress. She hadn't been phony with Abigail on their "fast-forward bonding day." When she'd said that the two of them had all the time in the world, she'd meant it.

So . . . why? There *was* some kind of countdown in Becky's life—but to what? She was always in a hurry. Why have a "fast-forward bonding day" if you had all the time in the world?

Abigail switched off the phone. Too hard to look at. Too painful. *Too fast, too fast*, she thought for the first time since boarding the airplane back in Glasgow. Instead, she stared straight ahead. Somewhere out there, she thought, somewhere beyond where the water blended into the horizon, was the world she had come from. A rainy, miserable, and awful world.

Only now did she wish she'd never left it.

CHAPTER TWELVE

BECKY JOHNSTONE'S BOOK OF REMEMBRANCE

Abigail painted the words, graffiti-style, as best she could. She filled each letter with bright colors using the brushes she had purchased right after the funeral. In the days since, she'd practiced on plain paper many times. Now she felt accomplished enough to do it for real.

Well. Close enough. It wasn't as easy as it looked, but the end result would have to do.

The idea had struck her on the sand dune. If Becky had taken her own life—and Grahame and Melanie and the police all believed with certainty that she had; the official investigation was now closed—then Abigail wanted to understand why. The more she thought about it, the more convinced she became that something terrible had driven Becky to it, something terrible *after* Abigail had seen her last. It was the only possible explanation. There had to be clues in the past, both recent and distant. So Abigail intended to get to know her sister from start to finish.

In truth, the deeper truth, Abigail also wanted something more than the iPhone as a memento. She had next to nothing to remember Nieve by. It was too late for her. But Abigail would fill this book with every detail she could find about Becky Johnstone. She would channel every ounce of that old robot precision into this one project. If she'd done this for Nieve; if she'd created something more meaningful—anything—that would help her remember, to celebrate, to grieve . . . then maybe she could be at peace with Nieve, too. Free of Nieve, if she were even more honest with herself. Free of Sophie, too. Would she ever be free of the mother she never knew?

Maybe through Becky, she could be.

This book would be Becky's biography, her legacy, her tribute. A way to cope with the tragedy. Closure. But, most important: a search for Becky's motive.

Abigail's eyes burned as she wrote the dates below the title, American style.

07-04-1994 – 05-08-2012

Less than nineteen years. Stray cats lived longer lives on the streets of Glasgow. *Billy* had outlived Becky. It wasn't right. Anger welled up inside her again. But she quashed it. Paint now dry, she turned to the first fresh blank page of the book. Ever methodical, she would start at Day One. For this, she needed assistance.

AT DINNER, ABIGAIL CHEWED on the gristle that was Melanie's beef stroganoff. All three labored over the food in silence, their new routine. Eventually Abigail gave up trying to eat and slid the lump of meat into her napkin.

"I was wondering if I could look at some of the things from when Becky was little," she braved. "Do you have photo albums? Her birth certificate?"

Grahame stared at her for a moment, perhaps surprised she'd spoken. "Of course." Dinner forgotten, he stood and retrieved a photo album from his den and waved her into the living room. "Come and sit with me for a while, come."

Melanie continued to eat, head bowed, as if she hadn't even heard the exchange. Abigail swallowed and nestled into the sofa beside her father.

He took a deep breath before speaking, his eyes on the album. "Listen, Abigail. I know this must be impossibly difficult for you. But I want you to know two things. The first is that you, here, now, becoming part of my life—it's a miracle. I cannot even begin to tell you how grateful I am. The second is . . . I want you to understand it's not your fault. Becky was—well, she was mixed up. But this had nothing to do with your coming here. Do you understand that?"

Abigail bit her quivering lip to stop the tears. "How can you be sure?"

"Here." He handed her a clean tartan handkerchief from his trouser pocket then drew another deep breath. "Let me tell you a story. Dennis—Mr. Howard—and I had a best friend at school." He flashed a bittersweet smile at the memory. "Ian Baker. Bakes. Inseparable from kindergarten. As teens we went a bit wild. Drugs, booze, tattoos . . . Dennis and I grew out of it. We were competitive academically, and we wanted to do something greater, something of service. I suppose it's what led me to the military. But Bakes, he floundered. Got kicked out of school. Turned to crime. He broke into a house when he was seventeen. His plan was to steal money for drugs. The woman who owned the house also owned a gun . . ." He didn't finish.

"Oh, I'm sorry."

"Yeah, me too." Grahame absently stared down the photo album. "He was so bright, so funny. He just got into the wrong things, didn't know when to stop, took it all too far. Of course we blamed ourselves. I gave him his first joint; Dennis showed him how to hotwire a car. Blamed ourselves like we're all doing here now. But the truth is, for Bakes and Becky, you can't blame anyone. All you can do is get on with things, to make sure people like them—unsettled people—have a chance, that they are given the right direction. So, no blame, okay?"

She nodded, wiping her eyes with the tartan. "Okay."

"Are you okay?"

"No." She managed a sad laugh through her tears. "Sorry."

"Please, don't apologize. I'm not okay, either."

Abigail glanced back into the dining room at Melanie, who'd begun clearing the table. She saw now why Becky called her the Stepford Wife. Her expression was grim, but not pained. If anyone exemplified robot mode, it was this woman. Abigail was almost envious.

"Melanie *is* okay," Grahame said, following Abigail's gaze. "She's tougher than I am. A tough cookie. She grew up in a trailer park, can you believe it? Parents died when she was fourteen. She keeps things on track. I'm so thankful to have her. I'd be a wreck without her, even if . . ." He swallowed. "And you. I'm saved by having you here. My lost little girl."

Abigail nodded. She was tempted to ask what brought his lost little girl here in the first place. Grahame never once addressed the subject of Sophie Thom. Not now, not with Becky, not since she'd arrived. Was it because Sophie fell into the Becky and Bakes category? Had Sophie been nothing but trouble for Grahame? Was the whole Socialist Workers Party thing his last foray into a wilder side he'd forsaken, or maybe even a noble attempt to save the woman he loved? Were the mixed CDs the last remnant of that effort to save her?

The questions died in Abigail's throat. Instead, she simply leaned over and hugged him.

He hugged her back.

It was the first time Abigail felt no awkwardness with her father. She didn't let go for a long time.

In her room later that night, Abigail opened the album Grahame had given her. The birth certificate was on the first page. *Name: Rebecca Sophie Johnstone.*

Born: 07-04-94, Western Infirmary, Glasgow.

Wow. Not only was Becky's middle name "Sophie"; she was born in the same hospital where Sophie had died. Three blocks from No Life.

Mother: Sophie Thom-Johnstone.

Father: Grahame Johnstone.

Weight: 7 lb. 10 oz.

Address: 18 Henderson Street, Hunter's Quay, Dunoon.
Siblings: X.

ABIGAIL SCANNED THE DOCUMENT on the printer Melanie had bought, reducing it so it fit the first page of her book. Pasting the back carefully with glue, she pressed it onto the paper. *Item one: completed.* The first photo in Grahame's album had been taken in France, or at least it looked like France; that was the Eiffel Tower, yeah? Becky must have been around two, chubby, rosy cheeked, and smiling broadly on a stone balcony—hotel room, probably—with the tower in the background. There were no earlier photographs.

So. Becky's first years were a gap, a void. She didn't want to ask Grahame about them. He had enough on his plate. She'd have to think of some other way. Maybe there was a pediatrician's file or something . . . As she was mulling, Abigail remembered what she'd stolen from No Life, what she'd stuffed in her Nike bag, what she'd never bothered to unpack. Not that she'd forgotten, obviously, but she knew the mere sight of it would make her sick and take her right back to Glasgow. Still, there was a chance it contained some information about her mother and sister. Biting her cheek, she reached up to the hiding place in the top shelf of her closet.

Down came the backpack, flopping on her bed. Her fingers felt damp and clammy as she unzipped it and removed the familiar orange file from the bottom of the bag.

ABIGAIL THOM.
50837.

A wave of nausea rose in her stomach. No matter what, no matter how far she got from Scotland, she would always be Child Number 50837.

The file was divided into sections: *Information. Correspondence. Reports.*

The *Information* section was just a list of facts: her weight and height (annual measurements), hair color, eye color, where she had lived, when.

Correspondence was similarly dull: letters about referrals, meetings, and financial considerations; there were also some loose telephone transcripts, stuffed in a folder in back.

She turned to the *Reports* section and began reading the first.

1. BACKGROUND
NAME: Abigail Thom
D.O.B.:   25-09-96
PARENTS: Sophie Thom (07-09-66)/NA
ADDRESS AT TIME OF BIRTH:
            27 Frederick Street, Peterhead,
            Aberdeenshire.
REPORT WRITER:
            JEAN MASON, GORBALS
            SOCIAL WORK OFFICE, OLD
            RUTHERGLEN ROAD, GLASGOW

1. BACKGROUND:

The sole existing report from Health Services indicates a home birth at the Frederick Street Address, without medical assistance. All other reports are missing or have been destroyed.

Health Services received an anonymous call at 23:11 on 25-09-96, complaining of loud noises from an anonymously rented flat. Authorities arrived to find both mother and infant physically healthy and determined the mother's identity to be Ms. Sophie Thom. Ms. Thom, however, appeared to be paranoid and confused, in addition to the birth trauma. The Emergency Technician recorded some of her statements, transcribed here:

"If he finds us, he'll take her like he took my first."

"The Navy is a front."

"This is about a drug."

"If we don't stop them, our children will not be our children."

Ms. Thom was unable to explain herself further, though it seems likely she was referencing her former husband and his job (Section 2). When Health Services attempted to visit a second time, as arranged, Ms. Thom had abandoned the Peterhead flat without leaving a forwarding address. She has not been seen since.

2. OTHER FAMILY MEMBERS

Health Services has since determined twenty-two months prior to the birth of Abigail, Ms. Thom gave birth to Rebecca Johnstone (04-07-94) at the Western Infirmary, Glasgow. The father was Ms. Thom's husband, Grahame Johnstone (19-04-65), a former officer in the United States Navy. His various ranks remain classified according to US Authorities.

Ms. Thom's erratic behavior appears to have surfaced shortly after Rebecca's birth. Psychiatric reports released upon court order (completed 12-11-95 when the family resided at 18 Henderson Street, Hunter's Quay, Dunoon) state that Ms. Thom was diagnosed with paranoid schizophrenia. She believed in a conspiracy: "a pilot project in its initial phases that is out to destroy our children." She insisted that her "husband and his friends be destroyed before everyone loses their minds." More significantly, she insisted that her concerns be recorded on paper. She repeatedly refused to take any medication for her illness, though she agreed to spend three months under observation at the Dunoon Psychiatric Clinic.

Law enforcement records indicate that she had attacked her husband on several occasions prior to her voluntary commitment. Grahame Johnstone never pressed charges. Testimony from the officers present indicates that he was cooperative and eager to help his wife manage her illness better.

On 29-03-96, Grahame Johnstone and Rebecca Johnstone departed Glasgow, Scotland, on Air France flight #405, bound for Paris, France.

According to the United States Internal Revenue Service, father and daughter have been living in Los Angeles, California, United States, since 15-04-96.

As far as mental health professionals were able to determine, Sophie Thom never told her husband that she was pregnant with their second child. She disappeared from Dunoon Psychiatric on 30-03-96. All attempts made to contact Mr.

Johnstone were unsuccessful. Addresses and phone numbers are unlisted.

3. CURRENT CIRCUMSTANCES

According to witnesses, Ms. Thom left Abigail in the care of Nieve Robson when Abigail was approximately three weeks old. Ms. Robson lived in a caravan at the anti-nuclear commune in Holy Loch, Argyll.

Nieve Robson died of cancer on 20-10-05, leaving Abigail without a guardian.

The guardian's death marks the first time Abigail Thom has come to the attention of the authorities since her birth. Yesterday, she was taken from the commune and placed in the care of the local authority. She is currently in Newar Park Children's Home, Argyll.

ABIGAIL TOOK A DEEP breath. *Newar Park.* She hadn't even remembered the name of that one. It was too much to take in. God, all this information; and she'd been told none of it. And Becky *was* in this file. That was the most horrifying part. Abigail should have known about Becky all along. Her sister had literally been hiding in plain sight ever since Nieve had died.

The report concluded with a bunch of typical legal shite: the Thom girl (*her*, a.k.a. The Unloved Nobody) should be taken into care on a permanent basis; contact with anyone on the commune should be prohibited . . . everything she already knew. Abigail bit her lip. Some social worker, this Jean Mason. Abigail couldn't even remember having met the woman.

Quashing the anger again, she reminded herself why she was doing this. She read the report once more. Her mother was a total bampot, as suspected. No wonder Dad had escaped with little Becky. No wonder he'd kept his address and phone number secret. He probably feared for their lives. Abigail felt another surge of warmth for Grahame, for the hard time he'd had of it back then. Her mum had attacked him. She'd set his car on fire. *Jesus.* Who could blame him for scarpering? Especially when he had no idea she was pregnant with their second baby.

On the second page of the Book of Remembrance, Abigail pasted in the OTHER FAMILY MEMBERS page of the report, highlighting Becky's address to the age of twenty-two months: 18 Henderson Street, Hunter's Quay, Dunoon, Scotland. There was nothing else to add.

Flipping through the photo album Grahame had loaned to her, she chose a few photographs to document the next nine years of Becky's life . . . what photographs she could find.

The album was so sparse. Her sister must have been around four years old in the photograph taken at Niagara Falls, on a boat with her father; both were dripping and laughing in oversized red NIAGARA TOURS raincoats. The next featured her in a yellow-checked school dress, standing in front of a city street. First day of school perhaps? But no, it didn't look like LA. From the movies and television shows Abigail had seen, it looked like New York.

Then nothing. Not a single shot for about six years. Grahame was clearly not the most sentimental guy in the world. But maybe guys who could "pull strings" and had to flee insanity weren't sentimental. Maybe that's the price Becky paid for a new life. Or maybe that's just what being raised by a single father meant. How the hell would Abigail know?

The next photo was taken at Edinburgh Castle when Becky must have been around eleven. God, they'd come to Scotland. So close. Becky wasn't smiling in this one. Hormones were probably kicking in. Nieve had died at around this time. Abigail's life was about to spiral into hell. And Becky was on holiday, just a couple of hours away. Abigail wondered if either of them had ever felt anything, dreamt anything, that didn't make sense. Maybe they were communicating with each other in a *Shining* kind of way, and neither of them realized it. She looked closely at the sullen eleven-year-old Becky. She had those same buzzing eyes. Were they reaching out? *Where are you? Are you there? Are you in trouble?*

But Abigail couldn't remember any possibly-telepathic thoughts or dreams. She was only nine. She was otherwise occupied with grief.

She slammed the photo album shut. She wasn't nine anymore. Now she could do something about it.

BECKY'S BEDROOM DOOR WASN'T locked. Abigail opened it quietly, careful to make sure no one heard her. As far as she knew, it wasn't out of bounds to enter her sister's room, not like the shelf of seventy-eights. Grahame and Melanie hadn't discussed it. Not even when the official verdict came in and the police tape was torn down—less than twenty-four hours after Becky's death. But still Abigail felt as if she were trespassing.

What was she was even hoping to find? Diaries, letters, toys, and trinkets? Left as they were? Isn't that what parents do when a daughter dies? Don't they leave her room preserved for all eternity? *Like as a rule?* Moving things, throwing things out . . . that would be too difficult. An impossibility, an insult. The room stays frozen in time: a solemn, sacred monument. Perhaps even a prayer that the child will somehow miraculously return.

So when Abigail flipped on the lights, her knees buckled.

Becky's room was stripped bare.

No trace of her sister's memory or anything else. The furniture, the clothes in her walk-in cupboard, the toiletries in her bathroom: all of it, gone. It had even been scrubbed. *Disinfected.* It smelled like her mother's hospital room in Glasgow.

Abigail's eyes burned from the stink and the glare of the lights against the barren white walls. Who'd done this? Why? And when? Had Becky's room been wiped out in the three days before the funeral, when Abigail had been unable to get out of bed? Not likely; there would have been noise, commotion. Besides, the police wouldn't have taken everything. No need when it was a cut-and-dry case of suicide. If there had been any suspicions about Becky's death, the yellow police tape would still be up and the cops would still be here night and day.

Grahame and Melanie did this. They did this and hid it from me. On purpose.

The realization stabbed at her, springing a leak. The warmth she'd felt for her father began to dissipate, faster and faster. Icy numbness filled the empty space. She could think of no reason why Grahame would want to erase Becky's entire life, so totally, so clinically. It wasn't overwhelming stress or an inability to cope. He'd sobbed in front of Abigail; he'd bared his soul with his vulnerability.

This didn't fit. It was off, creepy. The longer she stood in the hollow shell that had been Becky's oasis—for getting a "swerve on," for plotting with Stick and Joe, *for growing up*—the more certain she became that Grahame wanted to hide something about Becky's death. But what? Had he acted out of shame that his daughter was such a mess, or was it something deeper?

She raced downstairs and through the door that linked the house to the garage. Becky's van wasn't there. She ran into the front garden. It wasn't in the driveway either. In fact, she hadn't seen it since she'd last seen Becky alive.

"Grahame! Melanie!" Abigail yelled, darting from room to room in the house. She was furious. "Where are you?"

Melanie burst out from the laundry room adjacent to the kitchen, nearly slamming into Abigail in front of the vast stove. "Honey, please, there's no need to shout. What is it?"

"Where's all her stuff?" Abigail demanded. "Her room, her van . . . where's it all gone?"

"*Shh.*" Melanie gripped Abigail's wrists, her gaze never wavering. "Calm down. Your father's working in the den."

"What? Who cares? Where's all Becky's things?"

Melanie blinked. "Come here." She pulled Abigail into the laundry room, shutting the door behind them. "It's just how he deals with things. You'll make him upset."

"So he did it?" Abigail asked, raising her voice. "He cleared out her room?"

Melanie blinked again. Her eyes darkened. She straightened her neck. "We all have our ways of coping." The tone of her voice had changed: thin, serious, intimidating. Beneath the veneer of that pricey canary-yellow top and perfect blonde hair, a different character lurked.

Abigail took a small step back. "Okay. But what about how *I* cope with things?"

"Oh come on," Melanie hissed. "You didn't even know her."

What the fuck? The woman in yellow had peeled her face back, revealing a lizard alien. "You aren't being serious—"

"If you'd known her, you wouldn't be so upset," Melanie interrupted.

Abigail wanted to slap her. On the other hand, she was now genuinely afraid. If Grahame had been telling the truth, if Melanie was a trailer-park runaway, then Melanie was like Abigail. She came from nothing, which meant she was capable of anything. *A tough cookie.* Someone somewhere once had probably described Billy with similarly glowing words.

"How can you say that?" Abigail asked. "She was your husband's daughter."

"I'm sorry, that came out wrong," Melanie backtracked. She blinked again, and the lizard was gone. She crooked her neck, fake-smiley human back in place. "That was . . . I shouldn't have said that. Calm yourself down, pull yourself together. Your dad knows best, okay? Believe me. You don't know him very well. But I can tell you from someone who does know him, inside out, your dad knows what's best for him and for the people he loves. That includes you."

"*Melanie?*" Grahame's muffled voice called.

She leaned close to meet Abigail's gaze. "Don't say a word about this. Not a word, do you promise?" she whispered. She smoothed the wrinkles in the silky yellow fabric. Then she opened the door and yelled in her sweetest Stepford Stepmom voice, "*Coming, honey!*"

CHAPTER THIRTEEN

Back in her private bathroom, Abigail splashed cold water on her face. She looked in the mirror, casually at first, and then stopped to stare at the grim reflection. The water had darkened a few strands of hair. As always, anger heightened the glittering texture of her eyes. She *did* look like Becky. A bit, anyway.

If Grahame wouldn't help beyond a pathetic near-empty photo album, then she was on her own. But that was all for the best. Solitude was her friend; imagination was her enemy. She sat on the bed and logged on to the laptop Melanie had bought her.

For an hour or so she searched, but couldn't find Becky on Facebook or Twitter or anywhere else. She Googled her sister's name, but only found the same article she'd read in the airport: *Ex-naval officer Grahame Johnstone—married to actress Melanie Gallagher . . . daughter, Rebecca Johnstone . . . managing director of GJ Prebiotics in Los Angeles.* The last time she'd read this article she felt excited, nervous, full of anticipation.

She knew these people now. One of them was dead. Two were mysteries.

Then she remembered the iPhone.

Snatching it from her bag, she keyed in the pin number and scrolled through the list of contacts until she found Stick's name. He was supposed to be her closest friend. Maybe he had some of her things. Or at least she could try talking to him about what had happened here.

"Is that Matthew?" she asked in as good an American accent as she could pull off. She didn't want to be recognized.

"No. It's his father."

"Oh, is he there please?"

"No. I haven't seen him in three days."

"Really?"

"Nothing unusual." Mr. Howard's voice was surprisingly calm. "If you do see him, tell him I've washed my hands of him. I understand he's going through a hard time. We all are. But until he seeks my help and takes responsibility, I won't be bothered. Will you tell him that?"

Abigail opened her mouth to try to respond.

The line went dead.

ABIGAIL NEEDED MONEY FOR the taxi. She hadn't changed her remaining pounds into dollars yet. She felt bad doing this, but helped herself to $50 from the stash in a jar on top of the fridge. She'd repay it later.

She didn't have the address of the house, and it was getting dark, so it was difficult to remember how to get there. The taxi driver's patience wore thin as she squinted for landmarks and gave instructions: "This exit, here, quick . . . This way, no, no, turn left. Right at the lights!" She asked him to wait, but he drove off as soon as she handed over the money.

Night had now fallen completely. The street light had been smashed out in front of the ramshackle house, or *Headquarters* as they called it—by Stick and Becky in all probability. In the shadows, Abigail crept over the gate, along the side of the house, and into the back garden. The back door was locked. The windows were closed, the curtains drawn. Feeling around the gravelly ground with her hands, Abigail found a stone that was large enough. Holding her breath, she smashed the kitchen window.

A dog barked in the yard next door. No alarm sounded. She crouched, waited. The barking stopped. Thank God; no one had heard. Reaching inside, she felt for the snub on the kitchen door, opened it, and crept inside.

It was nearly pitch black. She wished she'd thought ahead and brought an electric torch. Not wanting to turn on the lights, she shambled around the kitchen, hands out before her, and swept surfaces until she found the cooker. The flame on the gas hob came on after three clicks, enough light for her to find a candle in the cupboard underneath the filthy sink. She lit it, and turned off the gas.

The hall was empty except for a few leaflets scattered on the grotty carpet. The bedrooms were bare, too. The living room, once a mess of papers and paint supplies, had been stripped and cleared of its furniture, just like Becky's bedroom.

Wait. A noise. What was that? Did someone cough? Was it the dog?

Abigail stopped still in the hall, shielding the light of her candle flame with her hand. She held her breath. Had she imagined it? She counted to twenty, slowly. Imagination was the enemy. She tiptoed, candle flickering before her, to the cupboard under the stairs. The lock was broken now. The door creaked as Abigail pushed it fully ajar. She moved a shaky hand inside the dark cupboard and watched as the weak candle lit the space. The box where Becky had stashed the money and her mother's photocopied letter was gone.

But the rectangular box they'd carried in from the van together wasn't. It was still covered in the blanket, untouched. Lifting the blanket slowly, she gasped.

The box was made of oak. It looked like a small trunk, or . . .

The lid was engraved with an image: two large birds, flying. *The chest.*

Abigail stopped breathing. The house went silent. There was only her heart, thumping under her ribs.

Nieve's chest of special things. Here. Now. In this place.

She covered her hand with her mouth. Her fingertips were trembling. In her other hand the candle flickered. Was she seeing things? How could that chest be in *this* cupboard? No, no, no . . . Abigail's breath came fast, terrified, as she felt for the chain around her neck. Nieve had given her the key. *Seven years ago.* Her father must have hidden the chest from Becky. Or not even hidden; as far as Becky was concerned, the chest was just another piece of junk in the attic. She'd probably never given a second thought to its significance. Why would she, if Grahame had lied? She'd only thought to grab an empty trunk, only when she needed storage space.

But there was no point in guessing about Becky. The chest meant that Nieve knew where Becky was, and that Nieve had kept her a secret from Abigail. When did Nieve send the chest overseas? The same day that she'd given Abigail the key, lying on her bed in the trailer, dying? *"Take this. Keep it with you. I don't have anything else to give you."* Those were Nieve's last words, pretty much. Until now, Abigail had always thought they were strange and wasted words. She'd always thought that Nieve might have said something more meaningful, more beautiful.

Abigail swallowed, her throat tight. She propped the candle against the door. It flickered into the wood. She felt for the clasp of the chain. She needed the key. Where was the small lever to undo it? *There.* Was that—

The candle toppled. *Shite.* The carpet was burning.

In a panic, she started pounding the smoldering carpet with her bare hands. *Damn it.* The flame died, but not before it singed her.

Tinkling. Footsteps on broken glass.

Panic turned to terror. Her imagination hadn't betrayed her, after all. She jumped to her feet. The noise had come from the kitchen. Someone was in the house. She tiptoed through the hall, stood behind the kitchen door, and peered through the crack with one eye. The back door was open. A dark figure was running across the back yard and jumping the fence.

Abigail bolted in the opposite direction—out the front door onto the street.

She didn't stop running until she reached a brightly lit bodega. A bunch of teenage boys stood in front of the door. Hoodies, bagged beers, drawn faces. They stared at her as she breathlessly called a cab. She stared right back. Funny: boys like this didn't seem so scary now. She wouldn't even know how to give them a scariness score.

WHEN ABIGAIL ARRIVED AT the house, Melanie was watching *Two and a Half Men* in the living room. She laughed along with the soundtrack. "Where have you been?" she asked Abigail without diverting her eyes. "I cooked Pad Thai."

For a moment Abigail wondered if the Alien Lizard was into dope, too.

TV and Pad Thai.

"I don't want to eat." Abigail planted herself in between Melanie and the screen. "I don't understand how you can— Hey. I'm talking to you."

"There's some left in the fridge," Melanie replied in a neutral voice. She tilted her head. Abigail's imagination was not her enemy here. Melanie was trying to see past Abigail to watch the screen. Melanie was truly oblivious to how her stepdaughter was a frazzled wreck.

With a shudder, Abigail hurried from the room and past her father's den.

Tonight, for once, the door was ajar. She caught a glimpse of him, sitting at the desk, head in hands. Abigail paused. She could feel the rage building. She would go in and confront him. She'd go in, any second now, and say: *"Hey, I wanted to see Becky's things, touch them, learn from them and you tossed it all out, like some old rubbish. Why?"*

Or: *"Hey, I found Nieve's chest. Which means Nieve knew where Becky lived all along. Which means you're a liar."*

Or: *"Hey, I want an explanation. Do you hear me? I have a right to know what's really going on. What is your wife's problem?"*

That's what she would have said if her father hadn't looked up. He spotted her fidgeting. His eyes hardened.

Abigail muttered a "sorry" and skulked her way upstairs. Melanie hadn't lied (she never lied). Grahame wanted to be left alone. And that was fine. Right. Because Abigail had learned something tonight. Grahame would never help her fill in the gaps. Who needed him, anyway? She'd never relied on anyone for answers and she was not about to start. She would wash her hands of her father, as Stick's father had washed his hands of *his* flesh and blood. She would find out everything she wanted to know without asking Grahame a single thing.

And without telling him a single thing, either.

CHAPTER FOURTEEN

The next morning at breakfast, Abigail refused Melanie's wobbly offering. "I don't like poached eggs," she said. She shot a glare at her father, hunched over his own untouched plate, his freshly shaved face inscrutable. "In fact today, I'm going to go looking for Marmite."

"Mar-what?" Melanie clucked her tongue. "I'll never understand that accent of yours. Will it fade, do you think?" She cleared away the uneaten eggs and tossed them in the bin, then refreshed Grahame's coffee. "And goodness, you're morphing into Becky. Breakfast is at seven . . . Look at you, coming down late, so sullen."

Abigail blinked. She wasn't sure what she was feeling. *Sullen?* Melanie had moved beyond 10/10 scary. Abigail thought of Camelia, more torn up over Billy's pathetic betrayal than Melanie was over her stepdaughter's suicide. *Trapped* was more like it. Frightened, maybe. Was there even a 7 A.M. breakfast rule? Now, still? And how could she mention Becky's name like an afterthought? Typically, Grahame seemed neither to notice nor care what Melanie said.

"Can I be excused? I'd like to go shopping."

Grahame nodded without looking up.

Abigail left the kitchen and walked straight to the front door, slamming it behind her.

HER FEET WERE BLISTERED and throat parched by the time she made it to Juvie. An hour and a half under an unforgiving LA sun: half on roads with no sidewalks. No doubt her neck and arms would turn a fiery red. She could already feel the burn. No choice but to walk. Most of her money had been spent on taxis the day before except a jumble of small bills and coins. The American change in her pocket looked and felt like play money compared to pounds: slender, green, and worthless.

New Beginnings, the sign outdoors read. She almost laughed.

She hadn't noticed it before. She'd hopped out of an expensive car when she'd last arrived. Just like New Life Hostel, right? Same euphemistic bollocks all over the world.

She pressed the buzzer at the front of *No* Beginnings Detention Center, gave her name, and pushed the huge, heavy steel gate.

"I'm here to see a boy called Joe," she muttered to the guard at the reception.

"Joe?"

Abigail thought back to the last time she visited with Becky. "Dixon, Joe Dixon."

"Ah, Joseph Dixon. Have you scheduled a visit?"

"Ach . . ." Abigail couldn't believe she'd come all this way to be stopped by petty bureaucracy. "No, I haven't. But he knows me. I'm Abigail. I'm Becky's . . . sister."

The guard looked up at her from above his glasses. *That look.* She was powerless scum again. "You need to schedule with us first. Are you on his list?"

"No, I'm not on his shitey feckin' list—" She broke off, biting her dry cheek.

But the guard smirked. He scratched his head. "That accent . . . Are you Scottish?

She looked up, hopeful. "Aye?"

His smile widened. "The only country on earth where a local drink outsells Coca Cola. And I don't mean Scotch."

"Heh. Good ol' Irn Bru." She tried to smile back. She felt her lips crack. What she'd do for a slug of the orange fizzy drink right now. Made from Iron girders, so the adverts joked.

"Do you ever go to the Barras in Glasgow?" he asked.

"Only if I wanna get stabbed." The Barras market was as depressing as it was hilarious. Only there, only in Glasgow, would stall owners try to woo passing customers by proclaiming: "DVD's only a pound: as advertised on Crime Watch!"

The guard peered at her over the rims of his glasses. "My mother is from a place called Pollok. Heard of it?"

"Pollok! Hell yeah. I have a friend from there." The word "friend" was a lie: Billy was from Pollok. And Pollok was the ugliest, most impoverished, and most dangerous part of the city. *More murders than people,* Billy once boasted. But she was getting somewhere with this guy; the right kind of small talk could cut through red tape, no matter how thick.

"Edna McGowan." He smiled.

"McGowan, aye." Abigail upped the accent-charm. "McGowans are well-known. There was one in my class." Not so much of a lie, this time, except that the word "class" implied school. Stacy McGowan had lived at No Life Hostel when she was sixteen. The same Stacy McGowan had died at No Life Hostel when she was seventeen.

"My mum's dead now, but I have cousins," the guard went on. "Rab, Jennifer, Chuggy . . . and Rhona, not sure which ones are McGowans."

Abigail nodded. She furrowed her brow. "Right . . . I might know Jennifer . . ." Of course she didn't know any of them.

"Really! If you see her, tell her hi from Uncle Jack."

"I will do," Abigail said quietly.

He was already buzzing her through the door.

AFTER AN OVERLONG STAY at the water fountain, she sat opposite Joe in the visiting area. His left arm was in a large plaster. He wore a sling. Injuries aside, he looked a lot better than he had the last time. His face had color.

"Hi, Joe," she said. "How's it going?"

"Broke my arm," he said with a dull grin.

"Sorry, I should've—"

"I was just being stupid," he interrupted. "I deserved it."

Abigail searched his eyes. They were clear, but the voice was off. He must have been on painkillers. "Do you remember me?"

"Yes, of course I do. Abigail. From Scotland."

"You know about Becky?"

"Yeah." He smiled sadly. "What a waste."

Abigail swallowed. "Are you okay?"

"I am." Nothing flickered behind that attentive gaze. "I mean, even with the broken arm, I'm feeling pretty good. You?"

"Fine. Listen, I was just wanting to find out more about Becky. Do you have any stories or photos or anything? It's just that I didn't know her—"

"Stories?" he interrupted again. "Let me think. I met her out on the streets. She liked my graffiti. She asked me if I wanted to join. They were wrong, you know."

"What do you mean?"

"They had it all wrong. She was unhappy. I'm not surprised she killed herself."

"What the hell?" Abigail spat. "Are you—" She stopped.

He shrugged. His vacant smile remained intact.

Goosebumps rose on Abigail's arms. She didn't know Joe very well—at all, really—but the kid she'd met the other night, the kid Becky was so desperate to rescue, was not the kid sitting in front of her. *I'm not surprised she killed herself.* It was Melanie déjà vu. He'd taken off his mask as the Alien Lizard Stepmom had done back in the laundry room. Only in Joe's case, the true face *was* a mask, the same mask Melanie usually wore.

"So, do . . . um, do you have any photos or letters?" Abigail asked. She wanted to get the hell out as quickly as possible.

"No."

"Have you seen Stick? Heard from him?"

"Matthew? No, he phoned after she died, said he missed her. They were close, those two. When they weren't hanging out together, they'd be texting or chatting on their phones all day."

Matthew. So now he was going all formal on her. Had to be prescription painkillers, right? Or maybe the room was bugged and he was paranoid. He'd been a lot more fidgety before. Nobody was that good an actor; she'd been around enough desperate or drugged people to know. The stare was blank, but focused. *On her.* The mask was reality. She turned away uncomfortably and looked out into the quadrangle. Last time she'd peeked through that window, boys had been laying into each other with knives. Now they were sitting calmly on benches, chatting.

"Quiet here today," she commented.

"It's amazing. You can make anywhere pleasant, anywhere, with a bit of positivity."

Abigail whirled back to him. This was Joe, wasn't it? This was the Juvie, wasn't it? Not only had Becky promised to spring him from this place—which wouldn't have been so hard, by the looks of it—she'd committed suicide by way of reneging. The memory of Nieve's funeral flashed through Abigail's mind, of being trapped against her will. Maybe this *was* an act. Maybe he'd planned something to honor Becky. "Have you been painting?" she asked carefully.

"Nah."

"They didn't give your stuff back?"

"Oh yeah, they did, but . . . I'm thinking of doing an apprenticeship."

"An apprenticeship? With a painter?"

"No." He laughed. "Plumbing. Honest work. I've got leaflets."

"Right." Abigail took a few quick breaths. "So you've not heard from Stick?"

"Beg your pardon? I missed that. Your accent."

"*Matthew? Have you talked to him?*"

"No, I'm through with him." He stood and extended a hand. "I should go back to my room. It's really cool of you to visit, though. Thanks."

Abigail didn't return the handshake. She accidentally knocked a chair over as she fled the room. The guard buzzed her through.

"What's going on here?" she hissed. Her fingers drummed the counter.

"I know, right?" the guard said. "It's great. Something in the water. Last few shifts have been the best I've ever had." He retrieved the phone Abigail had relinquished and handed it back to her with a laugh. "Pollok, Glasgow! Who'da thought it!"

ABIGAIL REMOVED HER SHOES for the walk home. There were some patches of grass along the way. Mostly the hot concrete burned the soles of her feet. She tried walking on her tiptoes. Sometimes she jumped from one discarded newspaper or shopping bag to the next, a lone frog on a toxic lily pond. The burning was better than the pain she felt when her blisters rubbed against her shoes. As far as the thirst, she tried to ignore it. Eventually, her mind filled with the familiar haze of drudgery. No need to go back to Glasgow, at least. This was just as bad, possibly worse.

Only once did something catch her eye.

A freeway overpass. *That* freeway overpass. The one she'd helped vandalize.

The billboard—where Abigail had held the ladder for Joe, where she'd tried not to admire Stick's photographs, where she'd cursed her sister's name—was blank.

Well, not quite. It was glued over with an advertisement for life insurance.

GRAHAME STOPPED HER WHEN she staggered into the front hall. His eyes swept her body from head-to-toe. "Good God, where have you been? What have you done to your feet?"

She opened her mouth. *Haven't broken in my shoes,* she wanted to say. All that came out was a croak.

"Why didn't you use the car service? Or call us?"

Before she could protest, he was rushing her into the kitchen and sitting her down in a cushioned chair. He ran a basin of warm water and filled it with antiseptic, lifting her ankles and dipping her feet in it gently. "This may sting a little."

"Ow!" She jerked her feet out with a splash.

"I need to take care of you, Abigail," he said. "I didn't take care of Sophie or Becky."

My God. He'd actually said her mother's name.

"You loved Sophie, didn't you?" she asked, squeezing the words from her dry throat.

He drew in a quick breath. "Your mother was a handful," he said. Once again, his tone became stern and distant. He grabbed a bottle of water from the refrigerator and handed it to her. "You're going to need Band-Aids on those blisters."

"Um . . . thanks." She stared up at him.

"I'm heading out for a meeting."

"Can I come?"

His eyes narrowed. "What? No. Why would you even ask?"

"I'm your daughter. You just said you have to take care of me."

"Abigail, you misunderstand. I'm sorry. This is a business meeting." He hurried from the kitchen.

Seconds later, the front door slammed behind him.

Abigail yanked her feet from the bowl. Melanie would have a fit if she walked in and saw this dripping mess, fouling up her kitchen. *Good. Let's see a fit.* Abigail hobbled for some towels in the cupboard, wrapped her bloody toes, and then plopped back down in the chair.

Grahame was right. She *did* misunderstand. He'd washed her feet, and then he'd washed his hands—of her. Just like Stick's dad. The fathers around here made no sense at all. Not that she cared. She pulled Becky's phone from her pocket and began to flip through the texts between Becky and Stick.

Stick: *be there at 10*

Becky: *he's watching my every move*

Stick: *sent you the file*

Becky: *i think Melanie was done*

Stick: *better move things to the house*

Becky: *this morning he begged me to keep away. cried.*

Stick: *tomorrow afternoon!*

Becky: *think someone's been in my room*

Stick: *we'll get him out. meet you at new begs at 7*

Before that last exchange, they read like gibberish. All but one, the day before Abigail arrived, from Becky: *he has a small box full of it in his den. he wants to do me. thinks it'll help. I changed it. like the taffy.*

Abigail chewed her lip. The first day, Becky had referred to Grahame's den as "the torture chamber." Was Grahame into…?

No, there was no point in going to such a dark place. Besides, she'd seen runaway girls at No Life abused at the hands of their fathers. None of what she saw here sounded the same warning bells. This was just plain creepy, for reasons she couldn't begin to guess.

There was only one video on the phone, the one she'd made with Becky. But there were dozens of photographs, all of the graffiti she'd done—up to that that last one with Abigail, signed with a large A at the bottom. Sliding her way from image to image, she counted seven works of "art" altogether. They were all exactly the same: faceless young zombies.

She checked the letters at the bottom.

One was signed with a "C."

One with an "R."

The next, a "G."

An "H."

Then an "O."

Last, an "N."

And, of course, the "A" at the sign she had helped with. Which was now gone. The images were in all kinds of places; they were huge and easy to see. Of course they were. It was the Graffiti Tease, the big new craze corrupting LA's youth, if Stick's father were to be believed.

Well, he could rest easy, Abigail thought bitterly. The Graffiti Tease was over. More than over. As she'd just seen with her own eyes, it was already being erased.

MELANIE MADE THEM THICK, rich, duck curry for dinner, with foul globs of jelly. If the stepmom was upset about having to clean the kitchen earlier, she didn't let on. The default-content-wifey mask was firmly back in place.

Abigail opted out of the charade. Besides, the stink alone was enough to keep her away. She had zero appetite. And Grahame was too distracted from his "business meeting" to complain about her absence at the table.

At her desk, she printed out the graffiti images and glued them into Becky's Book of Remembrance, one page at a time.

She found a picture of Stick online: a year-old Bebo profile pic, and stuck it to the next page. Weird; he was absent from Facebook and Google Images, just as he'd been absent from Becky's funeral. Was it deliberate? Was he trying to stay under the radar? Joe had much more material on him, most of it relating to his arrest. Several newspaper articles, in fact. "*Youth gets six months for vandalism and resisting arrest,*" read a headline. She cut and pasted the image of his face from that one, printed it, and stuck it on the page after that.

What next? She'd save the letter from their mother for last.

Only the rich need fire in their bellies. Becky had typed this on her computer the night she died. Abigail found herself scribbling the words on the blank page. Then she grabbed the phone and copied down the text messages, as meaningless as they seemed. Any scrap, no matter how tiny and strange, still added up to Becky's life.

be there at 10
sent you the file
he has a box of it in his den. I think he's going to do me. Thinks it'll help. I changed it.

On and on . . . From memory, she drew a picture of Becky's room as it had been before they cleared it. The desks, computers, bed, fridge, bar. Was she being silly, drawing pictures of the clothes she'd worn when they met? The crop top. The jeans. The belly-button jewelry—she'd never thought about it before, but the ring had a pendant: two tiny silver birds, their wings spread, free. Not unlike Nieve's . . .

Her heart squeezed.

Best not to think of Nieve now. Not until she had a chance to get back to that house, and to take a good look at what was inside that chest. *If* anything was inside. If it hadn't burned to cinders. She grabbed the iPhone and flipped over the graffiti Becky, Stick, and Joe had done, copying down the letters on a new blank page. They probably spelled something, right?

C.H.A.N.O.R.G.
C.R.A.N.G.O.H.
C.H.O.N.A.R.G.
N.O.R.G.A.C.H

In less than a minute, she'd driven herself crazy. The letters did not form a word. And, as far as she knew, the final letter had been painted. So, an acronym, maybe?

Come Hither All Nobodies Of Roaming Gnomes
No Ownership Reigns Green And Clear Help
Red Carpets On Hospitals Bring About Gangrene

She Googled "Graffiti Tease" and found hundreds of articles that had come out since the last letter was painted. Headlines included: *The final letter is A, but what does it mean?* And *Graffiti tease just a tease?* And, the most recent one—*I'll tell you what it means: Nothing.*

She almost laughed. What was the point? It was meaningless, all of it. But just as quickly a lump formed in her throat. Her eyes watered. She threw herself down on the bed and shook with sobs.

Becky was dead. Nothing she could do would bring her back to life. On the other hand, what else did Abigail have but Becky's death? If she had to live for the sake of ghosts, she would. She couldn't let Becky die like *this,* unmourned except for a sham funeral.

No. There were two things she needed to do.

The first was to figure out what was so important about her father's den. Why it was mostly kept closed, why Becky was so mysterious about it, why Becky had mentioned it in her text to Stick. And second, more importantly, she *had* to know what was inside Nieve's chest.

DINNER WAS LONG CLEARED, Grahame and Melanie safely shut in the master bedroom, when Abigail turned off the lights and prepared to head out.

Becky's iPhone suddenly buzzed in her pocket.

Abigail nearly screamed. Clamping one hand over her mouth, she sat back down on her bed and stared at the screen in the darkness.

One new message: *The world is crap without you.*

Sender Unknown.

Stick? She decided not to ring back. It might not be him, and if it was, he'd freak out, thinking it was Becky's ghost, or the police. Instead, she texted a careful reply: *This is Abigail. I'm alone. If that's Stick, can you pls call me*

The phone made her jump again when it buzzed a second later. She answered it.

He spoke quickly, accusingly: "Abigail, why have you got Becky's phone?"

"Hello to you too, Stick. The funeral was shit and I'm terrible and my father and step-mother have turned out to be aliens. How are you?"

"Sorry, I'm just . . . was just worried someone else had it."

"Well they haven't. I nicked it before my new father threw all her stuff away."

"Did he really?" His voice was different now. Sad. Not stressed and angry.

"You should have gone to the funeral."

"I couldn't. She would have understood."

It was so much easier this way, Abigail realized. Stuff just came out when you weren't face-to-face. "You were in love with her," she found herself saying. Rather: confirming.

"That was never gonna happen. I *loved* her, but it wasn't like that."

Abigail wasn't comfortable with her relief at the answer. It wasn't right to think about her own feelings when Becky had just died. But she did feel relief, and she *was* thinking about her own feelings. "You're right," she stated, fighting herself. "The world is crap without her."

A quiet "yeah" was all she heard next.

Abigail had never talked about anything personal over the phone. Landlines didn't exist on the commune. Cell phones were rare. And both were out of bounds or unaffordable in her life as an Unloved Nobody. But there was a larger truth, too. She'd never been close enough to anyone to *need* a phone. No reason to ring anyone and talk about her feelings. She'd seen intimate phone conversations on TV and movies, and it was . . . other-worldly. Frankly, it terrified her. Stick's voice was incredibly close, and loaded with emotion. She lay down on the bed and held the phone to her ear, pressing it against her, taking him in. "Where are you?"

"You're really similar to Becky, you know that? Upfront."

"'*Where are you*' is hardly a weirdly upfront kind of question."

"Ha. Different accent, but otherwise I could be talking to her."

"You're avoiding it, aren't you?" She wanted to know where he was sitting, what he was wearing. She wondered if he was lying down like she was.

"No, I'm not. Talk to me about anything."

He doesn't want me to know where he is.

She told him about visiting Joe, how weird he'd been, how he didn't seem like himself. She told him about the brutal walk to and from Juvie, and about the freeway sign, now covered with an advertisement. (She left out her righteous indignation that Becky's last Graffiti Tease mission had met with failure.) She hoped he'd say something to help her make sense of it all.

But he didn't give anything away. "Keep talking," he prodded.

She told him about her day with Becky, and how she felt she'd never been closer to anyone. "Silly, isn't it?" she finished in a jumble. "We only had a few days together."

"'Sometimes we had whole conversations without opening our mouths,'" Stick quoted.

Abigail's heart thumped. "*The Shining.* Right! That's exactly—"

"It's not silly." He cut her off. His voice caught. There was a pause and he coughed. "Nothing you say is silly."

She nodded. He couldn't see her, but she nodded all the same. She was on the verge of crying again, herself. "It's good to talk to you, Stick," she blurted out. She wondered if she should bring up what his father had said, or even that she'd spoken with him.

"Listen, I'd better go. But let's meet up tomorrow. Keep the phone safe. Delete the texts and logs. Don't tell anyone you spoke to me. Okay?"

"Okay."

"I'll text you tomorrow night," he promised.

"Right. Tomorrow."

She hung up and let out a deep breath.

What the hell was going on?

Curling into a fetal position, she pressed a pillow to her chest.

She replayed it all in her mind. She drunk in the bereaved warmth of his voice: "*Sometimes we had whole conversations without opening our mouths.*" Only a mixture of fear, guilt, and grief kept her from smiling.

CHAPTER FIFTEEN

At precisely midnight, Abigail pressed her ear against the door of the master bedroom. There were sounds. The TV? Maybe . . . ? She cringed. Not what she needed to hear, not from a father and stepmother, not *now*. Whatever. People in mourning did what they had to do. She'd read somewhere once (in an absurdly dry textbook that the sweet boy from Hillhead Library had shown her) that death could provoke a subconscious urge for intimacy. She'd giggled then.

She wasn't giggling now.

No matter. It didn't concern her. Even if Grahame and Melanie weren't watching TV, they were occupied. Tiptoeing along the dimly lit hall, she opened the door to the den.

She wasn't sure what she was expecting to discover. The room itself was boring: all in brown, ceiling-height bookshelves lining two walls, filing cabinets along another and a desk under the window. Everything was neat and sterile. Like Grahame himself. She peeked inside the drawers. Every file related to GJ Prebiotics: Accounts, Personnel, Meeting Minutes, et cetera, et cetera, yawn. Nothing interesting or suspicious. In the bottom drawer was what looked like a cooler, but too small for ice and a few pints. The silver padlock required a four digit code. A safe, perhaps? Probably money or jewelry inside. She rifled through his desk . . . nada.

Then she spotted a small crystal bowl. Car keys.

Abigail grabbed them, closed the door behind her, and hurried out the side door to the garage. The car's canvass top was down. She hesitated, then opened the door and slid into the driver's seat, sticking the key into the ignition—*Alarm! Bad idea. Shite.* She turned the key one notch back, as Becky had taught her during their driving lesson, and pressed SAT NAV.

The racket died.

With a sigh, she jabbed at LAST JOURNEY. If Grahame's meeting was so important that he couldn't include his lone surviving daughter, if he believed that she couldn't "understand" his "business," then that was his problem. Screw him. She would judge for herself.

An intersection and postcode lit up: *98564.*

She held her breath. Was there a noise? She whispered the postcode out loud so she would remember it: *"Nine-Eight-Five-Six-Four."* Sliding out of the car and closing the door as quietly as she could, she crept back into the house. Grahame and Melanie hadn't stirred. She rushed back into the den and dropped the keys back in the bowl. After grabbing another wad of cash from the jar on top of the fridge, she phoned a taxi.

Yes, she was technically stealing again. But why feel guilty? Melanie had told her: *this is your home.*

She scrawled a note and left it on the kitchen table.

Staying with my friend tonight. Back tomorrow. - A

IN THE TAXI, ABIGAIL phoned Bren. He answered on the first ring. She'd planned to apologize for the late hour, but he was wide awake. Music blared in the background. She sheepishly asked if she could crash at his place tonight instead of the Friday date they'd "diarized."

"Yippie!" was his response. "I'll make hot toddies."

"I may be a while. I have a few stops to make."

HALF AN HOUR LATER, she found herself staring at a warehouse in the middle of an industrial wasteland. *This* was where Grahame had driven for his meeting? Even the grizzled taxi driver seemed dubious. But the intersection and postcode matched.

She handed the driver some bills and told him to wait.

Thumbing her backpack straps, Abigail pushed through the open chain-link fence and began to circle the dark building. A few stray shafts of light poked through holes in a single battered side doorway. She peeked inside, on a brightly lit cavernous space, piled with neat stacks of blank cardboard boxes. Must have been around a thousand of them. There was a small office . . . and a man with his head down on the desk, asleep. His fat hump of a back rose and fell in an even rhythm. A security guard?

She tried the door; it wouldn't open.

After a quick hunt around back she found a shattered open

window and slithered through. She wasn't even sure what she was expecting to find. Nothing leapt out at her except the boxes, and the man—who, thankfully, was still snoring. She carefully tore open one of the cardboard lids. Inside were small clear plastic bottles filled with milky white fluid. She grabbed one and frowned at it. GJ PREBIOTICS.

A yogurt drink. What an idiot she was.

BACK IN THE TAXI, speeding toward Becky and Stick's hideaway, Abigail squirmed. She was annoyed. *A bloody yogurt drink.* Just as her father had said. There was also a second label on the bottle: PA23. Science gibberish, but the sequence seemed familiar for some reason? Perhaps she'd seen in it one of her textbooks. Or perhaps her stupid imagination was running wild again. That was the most likely scenario. She hadn't had a good night's sleep since Becky had died.

She shoved the bottle in the bag, tucking it under the Book of Remembrance. She stared at the street lights whizzing by the window, trying to think. There must have been a connection between Stick's promise to talk tomorrow—well, now today— and what she'd uncovered in her mission to celebrate Becky. *He nearly told me as much without telling me.*

Abigail almost spoke the last part out loud so she could hear just how idiotic she sounded. Her thoughts had become gibberish, too. A random sequence. She was lost. Truly lost. She had no idea where she was or what she was doing. LA was not Glasgow. LA was a mystery. LA was dangerous in ways even *she* couldn't imagine.

Before she knew it, the driver was pulling up in front of the ramshackle house. This time he refused to wait. "Here!?" he muttered. "Forget it."

He snatched her money and careened off into the night.

Well. At least she had Becky's iPhone.

She also had a flashlight, poached from the attic, which could make a handy weapon if anyone leapt out of the shadows. And she could always call Bren or Stick in a pinch and breathe to them her dying gasps. At this point, she was too exhausted to be frightened.

The kitchen window was still smashed. The lights were still off. Abigail crept once around the perimeter of the deserted house. Once she was absolutely sure she was alone, she darted inside and fumbled for the key around her neck. But as she crouched in front of the chest, she saw that the lock had already been broken. The lid creaked as she opened it with her free hand. The flashlight wobbled. She aimed the beam inside.

Empty.

Shite. She'd hoped and prayed that there would be something, anything. She slammed the torch against the chest. *Shite shite shite!* As fast as the anger consumed her, it dissolved. Now she felt guilt for lashing out. She would never damage this chest. Memories overwhelmed her: of Nieve dragging it out in the sun, of sitting on it and playing the guitar. She was a party-pleaser, Nieve, always choosing songs people could sing along to. "American Pie" by Don McLean and "500 Miles" by the Proclaimers. Abigail touched the velvet interior. This was as close as she would come to touching Nieve again—

There was a bulge. Underneath the velvet. Abigail aimed the beam and traced it with her finger. Something thin and rectangular was hidden in the lining. Using her key, she ripped at the corner of the fabric and tore it with her hand. A large white envelope fell to the bottom. Trembling, she shoved the torch in her mouth and tore it open. *A note from Nieve.* She swallowed hard. God, she hadn't seen that handwriting since the commune.

Underneath was a document, ten pages or so, stapled together.

Abigail read hungrily, pulling the flashlight from her mouth and holding it over the shaky yellowed notepaper.

If you found this letter, it means you found each other.

When is it? Years?

If you found each other, it's because Sophie knows it's time.

These are my last words, my beautiful, beautiful girls.

And I am smiling as I write them because you have found each other!

Be brave.

What you have to do now,

You have to do together.

Read this file carefully. It is not a small favor your mother and I ask.

It will be very hard,

Just remember—

What you do, you do for Sophie. Wonderful, glorious Sophie. Girls, believe me, your mother is the most incredible person I have ever known and she loves you both with all her heart. And what you have to do now, you also do for silly old Nieve.

You do it for happiness.
But most of all, my ever-majestic birds,
You do it for freedom.

Abigail's eyes stung as she read. She sniffed and wiped her nose with her sleeve, slumping down on the floor beside the chest. Yet she also felt annoyed. For once, could someone leave her a letter that made sense? She put the note aside and glanced at the stapled document.

Stamped in red on the front page were the words TOP SECRET. She flicked to the next page.

THE GRANOCH PROJECT
1996

The words leapt off the page. The letters on Becky's graffiti were not an acronym, and they did not spell chanorg or crahgoh or chonarf or norgach or crohbag.

GRANOCH.

She read on. *The pilot project was implemented in 1996, in the small town of Granoch, Argyll, Scotland.*

Of course! How could she have forgotten Granoch, the housing estate just north of Holy Loch? Several of her classmates in Dunoon came from this town. Nothing more than four 1960s council house buildings, each twenty-two floors high. The township loomed over an otherwise picturesque area, an ugly reminder of the fractured state of the country. Single-parent families, drug users, alcoholics, the mentally ill, the infirm—all had been moved there from Glasgow in the 1960s. Better conditions improved their lives at first, but then it all fell apart. Isolated, deprived, and disenfranchised, no one in their right mind ever stepped foot inside Granoch.

Once, Abigail had asked Nieve if she could play with a classmate who lived there, excited at the idea of going all the way up to her flat on the nineteenth floor. Nieve had suggested the friend come to the commune instead. "It's a terrible shame, but it's not safe there, darling," Nieve had said.

The friend's mother had said she wasn't allowed to go for a playdate at the commune either. Part of being "looked after" by the local authority was being shunted off to Granoch Residential School at the age of fourteen for a month or so, a jail-like building with jail-like rules. Funny, perhaps she hadn't recognized Granoch in the graffiti tease letters because she'd repressed the shit-hole, burying it as deeply in her mind as she possibly could.

No. It wasn't funny at all.

ABIGAIL HAD NEVER HEARD the sound in real life before, but she recognized it immediately. A trigger, clicking ready.

The cold steel of the barrel sent waves of adrenaline through the back of her neck. She wanted to run, but knew she shouldn't. She froze.

"Move and I'll shoot," the voice behind her warned.

"Okay." Abigail gripped the letter and report, her hands trembling.

"I . . . I'm . . ." The gunman seemed nervous, unsure what to do next. His voice was also strangely high-pitched. "Get down on the ground, face down."

Abigail stretched her legs out behind her, and her hands

out in front, papers in hand. The torch was still lit, pointing directly at the gunman's feet. He wore bright orange Adidas trainers with blue stripes.

"Stay on the ground and count to two hundred . . ." The voice seemed to run out of steam. "Abigail?"

She'd seen these shoes before. "Stick? Is that you?"

Feet on glass. Someone else was in the house. Before Abigail knew it, Stick was hauling her to her feet and dragging her out the front door.

"This way," he said. He turned left at the front gate.

Three men in suits, all with guns, raced out the front door after them.

"Here!" He grabbed her hand and ran across the road into a dark lane.

A yellow mini was parked at the end of the long dark alleyway. Tossing the gun in the back of the car, Stick jumped over the door into the driver's seat. Abigail hurled herself in after him. She tried to grab her seatbelt, but couldn't find it. Stick screeched left onto the street.

Abigail found herself wondering why on earth Stick was driving a bright yellow car and wearing luminous orange trainers. If he was involved in all sorts of illegal shenanigans, surely he should wear something more discreet. Stick drove through a red light, groping for her belt with one hand. A black car was following them.

"Shit, Abigail," he muttered. "What were you doing there? You're dead now. We're all dead now. Where can we go? There's nowhere safe."

"You have a *gun!*" she yelled.

"Not real. Water-gun look-alike. Banned now. I mean, you can actually cock it, like you're about to shoot. You know, even though the hammer doesn't do anything."

The black car was gaining on them. Stick pressed hard on the accelerator, winding his way through wide streets, then narrower ones—eventually reaching an area with tiny laneways that backed onto a canal. Car chase scenes in movies (the few she'd seen) bored Abigail. Screeches and near misses, buses turning over, drawbridges opening up at the right or wrong time, fruit stalls smoothied, cop cars bursting into flames . . . a load of boy nonsense.

This was not boring.

Only afterward did it seem like slow motion. Or perhaps it really did happen in slow motion. Certainly time slowed down. Stick's yelling "Hold on" came out like: "Hooollllddddd Oooonnn," facing her as he turned the wheel to the left. There was nothing to hold. She dropped her papers, fumbled around to find something she could grab. She didn't have her seatbelt on and the swerve almost catapulted her out the window. Left hand on the wheel, Stick grabbed her shoulder with his right and stopped her flying out the side of the car.

"Belt . . ." he said, and she reached for it and clicked it in.

They were heading for a very narrow alleyway. They were going to crash. They were going to die. They lost the side mirrors—the scrape was deafening outside her window. She breathed in and out quickly, and then turned to look behind her. The black car was too wide to follow them. It had ground to a halt. The men inside the car couldn't open their doors to get out.

Thank God. As Stick kept driving, Abigail took note of the number plate and said it out loud: "4DMSP38."

Stick still had his arm around her, perhaps because she was shaking. Or he was in shock, frozen. Sound and movement returned to normal speed. They drove away from the black car and headed along a waterway.

"Is this the Venice Canals?" Abigail asked.

"Yeah," Stick said. Her question caused him to remove his arm. She wished she'd remained silent.

"I know where we can go."

WHEN BREN FINALLY CAME to the door, he was dressed in shorts and a shirt, which he hadn't done up. If Abigail hadn't been preoccupied with the fact that three men with guns were after her and the most beautiful man on earth had just put his arm around her, she might have taken more notice of his really-quite-incredible six-pack.

"Abigail! Oh, you've brought a friend."

"This is Stick. I'm sorry . . . Can we come in?"

"Um. Sure . . ."

"And is there any chance we could park in your garage?"

THE YELLOW MINI SAFELY tucked away, Abigail and Stick sat at Bren's kitchen table as he heated up the saucepan of hot toddies he'd made earlier.

"So," Bren poured some into cups, a look of amused disbe-lief on his face, "what you're saying is that a secret agency . . ."

"The Granoch Group," Stick explained. "It's made up of guys who were screw-ups as teenagers, like my dad and Becky's—Abigail's." In the bright kitchen light, Stick looked gaunt, like he hadn't eaten for a while. He was definitely annoyed that Bren seemed so reluctant to believe him. He continued, trying to sound as calm and as sane as possible. "They think they can actually get rid of those screw-up urges with meds. Some kind of guilt, regret, and repentance maybe, I don't know. I think in Abigail's dad's case he felt guilty about a friend who died."

Abigail nodded. "Bakes, he told me. Got into drugs and burglary."

"Probably one of his reasons for getting involved," Stick confirmed.

Bren took a sip of his hot whisky and honey drink. He flashed a weak smile. "Abigail, are you actually buying all this crap?"

"I am," she said. "Becky died last week. They say she killed herself but now I'm not sure. Her death wasn't right. Things aren't right."

"Oh my God—your sister died?" Bren set his mug down and put his arm around her. "You should've called me. Of course things don't seem right when you lose someone you care about. But look at me, look. He's talking like a nutcase. Who is this guy exactly?"

"I'm not a nutcase," Stick said.

Abigail clung to Bren for a moment. Her life in Glasgow had taught her to be wary, especially of men. Even Billy had seemed charming at first, and all he wanted was to draw her into his junkie brothel. She stared at Stick now. He could be anyone. She already knew he lived two lives. Maybe he lived several. Maybe at least one of them was dangerous and sinister. Shit, she had let her guard down. She was turning into a gullible idiot. And then it dawned on her. Stick could have killed Becky: unrequited love turned to jealous rage. She couldn't see evil in the eyes that were now pleading with hers to believe him, but this meant nothing. To be a good liar, you must be good at hiding. Maybe Stick didn't go to the funeral because he was a murderer on the run, which was why men with guns were after him.

"But you're suggesting Becky was killed by her own father?" Bren asked Stick.

It sounds crazy, Abigail thought. The desperate accusations of a guilty psychopath. She noticed that his leg was shaking.

"No," Stick said. "He knew what she was up to, but no, he wouldn't have wanted her to die. He loved her. I think he had other ideas about how to stop her. But he's not the boss."

"Who is the boss?" Bren asked. He almost sounded amused as he sipped his drink again, one arm still around Abigail.

"I don't know," Stick began. "I . . ."

It came pouring out of Stick's mouth in a mad jumble: he wasn't a nutcase; he and Becky had found out about the Granoch Project six months ago. Stick had been writing an essay when the computer crashed and he'd lost all his work. A random search included an email his dad sent to Grahame about the PhD he did at UC Berkeley on neurological-pharmaceutical intervention to antisocial behavior in monkeys.

"They're trying to control us," he finished.

Abigail blinked several times. The guy was talking about naughty monkeys. His leg shook faster.

"Excuse me, but what on earth does your father's PhD and monkeys have to do with anything?" Bren asked, echoing Abigail's thoughts.

"My dad is smart," Stick spat back. "Smarter than any of us."

"A dastardly secret organization!" Bren exclaimed. "Are there code words and hidden headquarters? Abigail, this guy is nuts . . . you see that, right?"

Abigail turned to Stick. His forehead was beaded with sweat. But so was hers.

"I know it sounds ridiculous, but listen to me," Stick pleaded. "The Granoch Group thinks they can cure bad behavior. They came up with a tiny implant that you inject into the inner arm. The drug itself is like an anti-depressant—a serotonin reuptake inhibitor—a happy pill, only much stronger, and semi-permanent." His eyes bored into Abigail's. "You found something important in the chest, didn't you? All those years, Becky thought it was empty. I saw you reading something about the Granoch Project. Can I have a look?"

Abigail swallowed. She handed him the report she'd clung onto since fleeing the ramshackle house. Stick flicked through it and began reading from the second last page.

"When first tested on 1991 Monkey Group A (Given the implant) varied from Group B (No implant) in the following ways:

> *increase in socialization*
> *increase in cooperation*
> *decrease in libido*
> *less aggressive behavior*

"These effects are already apparent in 1996 Human Group A.

"Further work is required to decrease the size of the implant; to increase the lifespan of the implant from its current level of six years; and to induce the initial effects more rapidly, which currently take an average of two days. It is also necessary to monitor the negative side effects experienced by Monkey Group A and Human Group A, namely weight loss (45%) and in the case of Human Group A, a potentially life-threatening psychosis (2.5%). It is suggested that the other significant side effect—loss of libido (95%)—should be considered a positive outcome and perhaps developed so that sexual urges are reduced even further."

The report made Abigail feel queasy. No one, *no one*, except Abigail herself, should have the right or even capability of reducing her sexual urges. "But, what does any of it have to do with us?" she said, taking the report from him.

"They had a plan to roll this out," Stick muttered. "Becky and I were going to expose it."

Bren banged the saucepan down on the table. "What are you *on* right now?"

"Sorry?" Stick asked.

"I don't even know your real name, *Stick!*" Bren shouted. "Are you acting like Harrison Ford to impress Abigail? Nice job. I can see that it's working."

"This isn't about Abigail. It's about Becky. And Abigail knows it." Stick's eyes moistened. "Why would Becky have killed herself? Think about it. I've never known anyone with such purpose. She didn't want to die."

Abigail blinked between the two of them. Bren had a point. But none of that really mattered. She had all the information she needed now. Either Stick was a madman, or three madmen were after them. Either way, she needed to call the police. As calmly as she could manage, she walked over to the kitchen bench, grabbed the phone, and began to dial 9-1-1.

The kitchen window collapsed in a burst. Its shards of glass clattered into the sink, a violent tinkling house of cards. At the same moment, Abigail heard a crack on the wall behind her. There was a ringing in her ear. She turned toward Bren, who was staring in wide-eyed horror at a tiny, smoky black hole in his wall. Another *whizz* and *crack:* this one closer to her head. Another hole appeared in the wall.

"Down!" Stick yelled, tackling her.

Bren dropped his mug and fell to the floor, too. Abigail wriggled free from Stick. On her hands and knees she inched toward Bren, whose face had turned a ghastly white.

"The police wouldn't just shoot at us like that," Stick whispered, his voice shaking. "You have to believe me."

Bren gaped at Abigail and nodded. He was thinking what she was. Somebody was trying to kill them, and it wasn't the cops.

"I know a way out," he gasped. "Keep quiet. Follow me."

Abigail grabbed her backpack and crawled after Bren, with Stick right behind her, out of the kitchen and to a back door in the living room. "On the count of three follow me." Bren stood up and gestured for them to do the same. "One . . . two . . . *three!*" He flung the door open, sprinted across the small courtyard garden and jumped the fence that bordered the canal. A small speedboat was moored to a rotted wooden post. Abigail followed, crouching down as she ran. Bren had the engine running even before Abigail and Stick managed to jump in.

"Move it!" Bren commanded.

The front of the boat edged skyward with a sudden jolt. Abigail's butt hit the seat hard, but she didn't feel any pain. Stick teetered beside Bren at the far end of the boat, near the engine. In a haze of adrenaline, she turned back toward the house. The three men in black suits were now running across the garden and jumping the fence.

One of them aimed and fired a shot.

Stick winced. His eyes widened, as if in disbelief. Abigail could only watch, not quite fully processing. He clutched at the side of his belly and fell backward into the water.

Without thinking, she jumped in after him.

The dark, lukewarm water closed over her head, heavy with

the stink of gasoline from the boat's engine. She thought she heard Stick gasp, but was suddenly fighting for her life in a panic. *I can't swim. I can't swim. Becky, where are you now?* Her legs and arms were moving in all the wrong ways. She sank, managed to surface once or twice, and then sank again. A strong pair of hands reached under her arms and lifted her back into the boat. She sputtered, choking on the polluted canal water she'd half-breathed, kicking in protest.

"No! No, put me down. We can't leave him!"

Bren gunned the engine.

Her wet feet slipped out from under her. The last thing she remembered—before her head cracked against the side of the boat—were police sirens, wailing in the distance.

CHAPTER SIXTEEN

Big, bad, dangerous Glasgow. Bad, ugly social workers. Ugly Billy. Camelia. Get her away from there. Save her from No Life. Kelvingrove Park. Glasgow University. Holy Loch. The caravan. Strange man at strange funeral. Throwing stones into Loch Lomond. They're all dead. Granoch. I'm an Unloved Nobody. Billy! Billy is here, now, somehow . . . "What you sayin'? What you talkin' about, hey? Hey, honey?"

Abigail opened her eyes. Bren was gently brushing her fringe. "You hit your head in the boat. But you're gonna be okay. Stop talking about big bad things. You're safe now. I'm here."

"Where am I?" Abigail sat up and pressed her hand against her throbbing skull. She was sitting on the lower shelf of a bunk bed, right next to Bren, in a very small space. A moving space. The hard mattress rumbled and bounced beneath her. The top of her head grazed the top bunk. A bus or train? There was a window behind her, a highway receding.

"You're safe. Mom and Dad picked us up."

Right. *Bren's parents own a Winnebago and are enjoying*

retirement. The words clanged in her head, an advertising bro-
chure based on some distant memory: scenes of the happy,
drunken chat she and Bren had shared on the plane. Then all
the rest of the memories came flooding back in terror. "Oh my
God, Stick! He's in the canal! We can't—"

"He's gone." Bren interrupted. "It wasn't your fault. There's
nothing we could do."

"Is he dead?"

"I don't know. He didn't resurface."

She nodded. Her throat was dry. There were other memories
now. The photographs Stick had shown her while she'd held the
ladder at the freeway sign; the party where she tried hard not to
feel what she was feeling; his hand on hers as his yellow mini
screeched through a narrow alleyway. Most of all: doubting him
in Bren's house when all he was trying to do was save her life. "Is
he dead?" she whispered. The pain in her head seemed distant.

"Shh." Bren said. "It's not your fault."

"You shouldn't have left him."

"I had to. They'd have killed you." He had tears in his eyes.
He touched her face. "You nearly died back there." He kissed
her forehead and moved his lips down so they were just mil-
limeters from hers. "Oh Abigail . . . thank God—"

"Hiya . . . Can I come in?" The small plastic door opened
without a knock.

Abigail turned to the woman standing before them. The
Scottish voice, the shape of her figure, the flowing skirt and red
hair and craggy freckled face: this was Nieve, reborn. She felt
herself letting go, becoming wee Abi, just eight years old, wee

Abi who didn't have to be a robot, who could cry when she was upset knowing that Nieve would listen to her and comfort her. She opened her arms to Nieve—but it couldn't be Nieve—and sobbed into her shoulder.

I'm delirious. I've hit my head and I'm delirious.

"I'm sorry," Abigail said. "It's just, you just remind me of someone." She took a deep breath and wiped her eyes.

The woman patted her shoulder. "How's that noggin?"

That's right: Bren's mum is from Scotland.

"I'm fine but, please, we have to go back." Abigail peered past her through the open door: a tiny kitchenette on one side, bench and table opposite—and at the front, a driver with a head of grey hair. The woman handed her a glass of water.

"Thanks Mrs . . ." Abigail couldn't remember Bren's last name. Did she even know it?

"Gracie, call me Gracie. Drink some water first," she said. "That was some wallop you got, hen."

"There's no time . . ." Abigail slurred her words. She felt woozy.

"How is she back there, eh?" the male driver at the front yelled. "She okay?" His accent was Canadian, like Bren's.

"She's gonna be just fine!" Gracie yelled back, handing Abigail two white tablets. Her eye twinkled. "I know Bren is relieved. Though I'm not sure I approve yet."

"Mom, please," Bren growled. "Let's not start."

Abigail swallowed the pills. "What do you mean?"

"You're still in high school. When Bren told us about you . . ."

"Wait. What are you talking about?"

Gracie glanced at Bren, who shook his head. "Oh, God.

It's happening again, isn't it? Please don't tell me you think I'm gay."

"You're not?" Abigail cried.

His mother sighed, a wistful grin playing her lips.

"We need to go back and find Stick," Abigail gasped, clinging to the one truth she thought she understood. But she could no longer keep her eyes open. She fell asleep almost immediately.

WHEN SHE WOKE, THE Winnebago was still. The small bedroom area was dark. She sat up carefully, her head still sore, but the pain had receded. She glanced out the window. They had stopped in an empty car park next to a beach. She could hear the waves crashing at the foot of the cliff. Hunger gnawed at her stomach. Her jaw tightened.

She shouldn't have fallen asleep. She should have been trying to get an answer about Stick. Was he dead? How much time had she wasted? She had to get her head together, make a plan, and act. Fast. She threw open the door.

Bren and his mom sat across from each other at a tiny plastic kitchen table, Gracie at a laptop. Bren's dad stood at the opposite wall, a marker in hand. They turned to her. Abigail opened her mouth, and closed it. Several large sheets of flip-chart paper had been pasted to every available space: arrows, maps, and photos. The grey Nike backpack, the letter from Nieve, the social work file, Becky's iPhone, and the yogurt drink Abigail had stolen from her father's warehouse . . . all were lined up on the table between Bren and his mum.

Bren's father was the only one who moved. With his long

hair and AC/DC T-shirt, he looked more like an aging rock star than an ex-homicide detective. He capped his felt-tip pen and held out his hand to shake hers. "I'm Craig McDowell."

She shook his hand. "Listen . . . thanks for everything, but these are my things."

"We're just trying to work out what's going on," he said.

"Have you called the police?" she asked.

"Not yet."

Abigail felt herself slipping back into robot mode. She trusted Bren. And okay: his family had rescued her. And okay: so Gracie seemed to have something of the lovely Nieve about her. But she didn't know them and they shouldn't have been rifling through her things. "Right. Well if you don't mind, I'll just gather all this up and head off to the police station."

"I'm sorry," Gracie said. "We didn't mean to upset you. But we think we should wait before doing that. You know, in case it's not safe."

"Why wouldn't it be safe? Weren't you cops?"

"That's right," Craig stated. His voice was far more authoritative and strident than his son's. "I was a cop. And three men just attempted to kill our son. We want Bren, and you, to be safe. We want to help. We need your trust."

"They are the good guys," Bren said.

Abigail didn't answer. Did she even believe in good guys anymore? Not really, except for Bren himself. But she needed all the help she could get. Yet again, she'd landed in an unfamiliar place with a new set of strangers to negotiate. She pulled her short fringe back with her hand, sighed, and studied the sheets of flip-chart paper stuck on the walls. Gracie slid over and patted the bench beside her. Abigail remained standing.

"The best ammunition is information," Craig said. "Whatever happened to Stick has already happened. Another half an hour won't change that. Before we do anything, read over all of this carefully," Craig instructed. "Maybe you'll see something we haven't."

She first noticed the photo of the Granoch Group. Abigail examined the picture. That was Grahame Johnstone, right enough. Much younger, but just as uptight and stern. The only difference was that his hair was natural brown, rather than dyed. She then read the entire document on the Granoch Group, focusing, taking her time, remembering the key points:

* Granoch Group – committed to addressing deviant teenage behavior.
* In 1996 they launched the Granoch Project, which involved adding a drug called PA23 to the routine shots given to fourteen-year-olds in the Granoch area. PA23 immunized against discontent, curing urges that cause individual unhappiness and contribute to social decay.

Abigail picked up the bottle of Prebiotics she'd stolen from the warehouse and studied it. The four digit code on the front was . . . PA23. She must have buried this deep in her unconscious too. It was the Dunoon and Granoch postcode.

It wasn't a Prebiotics drink. It was a drug.

"PA23. I lived with Nieve in that postcode," Abigail heard herself say. "Holy Loch, in Argyll." She opened the bottle and examined the liquid. There was a tiny capsule inside. They must have developed it to make it so small it would be undetectable. So small it could be ingested along with the innocuous liquid.

Next, Abigail looked at some information Bren's family had collated onto a table about Granoch, using information from social networking sites like Friends Reunited and Facebook.

GRANOCH 1996 *PA23 (Human Group A)*	**What was the sample group like?** *Aged 14* *Serious trouble-makers—drugs, car theft, violence, gangs.*
GRANOCH PRESENT DAY *Human Group A*	**What are they like now?** *Aged 31* *Electricians, plumbers, nursing assistants, etc., married with kids, on Neighborhood Watch.* *All law-abiding citizens*

GRANOCH 1996 *Non-Sample Group* *(Not given PA23)*	What were they like? *One year older – 15 years old* *Serious trouble-makers – drugs,* *car theft, violence, gangs*
GRANOCH PRESENT DAY *Non-Sample Group*	What are they like now? *In prison, gang wars, murder,* *overdose, suicide* *One rags-to-riches story* *Teenage pregnancies*

"But . . . is that bad?" Abigail said, after taking in the information on the table. "Who'd want to end up stabbed or in prison?" From what she'd seen so far, she couldn't help think that some of it made sense.

"Of course it's a bad thing!" Gracie snapped, outraged. "Abigail, you'd have been a prime candidate. The bright, passionate, angry girl next to me—gone! This is about poverty and nothing else. Should only the rich take risks, have fire in their bellies?"

Abigail stared down at her feet. "Becky wrote something about fire in bellies once," she murmured. She could almost see her sister now: sitting at her desk the night before she died, intense and purposeful, tapping away at the keyboard. It was all too much. Abigail needed time alone to focus. "Can you give me some time alone with all this, just ten minutes or so?"

"Of course," Bren said. He led his parents out the narrow trailer door.

She started with the familiar orange social work file: #50837. She flipped to the back, leafing through the small pieces of paper with names and numbers on them.

GP appointment. *Boring.* Education Board. *Boring.* It angered her that she'd been deprived of all that, especially in all the insanity surrounding her departure from Scotland, but the worst by far was the last scrap of paper she found.

For: Abigail Thom

From: (Refused to give name. Male.)

Tel: (Not given, but did 1471 to retrieve – 555 78450234)

Message: Mother gravely ill, requests Abigail visit at Western Infirmary. Urgent.

So it wasn't the hospital who'd phoned. It was someone else. And Unqualified Asshole hadn't told her about this message. Useless prick. Without pausing to think, she used Becky's phone to dial the UK telephone number.

An interminable *buzz-buzz* followed with a dull: "Hullo?"

"This is Abigail Thom," she said. "I'm ringing because someone left a message for me using this telephone number."

She waited through the long pause. Perhaps the person didn't live there anymore. Perhaps the message was from someone at the hospital after all.

"Abigail?" a man's voice finally said. "Is that really you?"

"Who are you?" she asked.

"My name's Harry. Harry Belwood. You don't know me, but oh, I know you. Sophie's little Abi. Where are you? Are you okay?"

"How do you know me?" she pressed.

"I'm . . ." He hesitated. "Your mother was the love of my life." With that, he started jabbering, revelation after revelation, each more confessional than the last. But it wasn't that her mother had been in a long-term, loving relationship that shattered Abigail's view of her past. It wasn't that the couple had lived a quiet life together on a disused quarry in the Scottish Borders for fifteen years. Or that this man was the "Next of Kin" who had requested Sophie's ashes, and scattered them in the Holy Loch. Or that he was the blond man she'd seen at the funeral. It was how he finished: "She thought about nothing but you and Becky, all her life."

Abigail couldn't answer. She squeezed her eyes shut. Then she breathed. "Yeah, well how was I supposed to know that, Harry?"

"She was consumed with grief and worry. She was in danger. She knew she couldn't make contact with either of you, for your own safety. It killed her, every day."

"Well, why didn't *you* get in touch?"

"Sophie begged me not to," Harry said.

Abigail nodded. Her throat was too tight to speak.

"Sophie never misled me, so I promised," Harry said. He was crying, too, now.

"I have to go." Abigail was desperate to find out more, but the clock was ticking. She just couldn't stay on the phone.

"But before I do, I have to tell you something. Something really awful . . . Becky died. Suicide, they say, but I don't think that's what happened."

"What! Oh, God, no." His voice quavered. "I'm coming over."

"No, don't come, not yet," she warned. "But tell me something, did Sophie say why we might be in danger?"

"No. I knew better than to press her."

"So you haven't heard of the Granoch Group?"

"The what?"

"Have you ever heard of PA23?"

"Is it a postcode?"

"Okay, forget I said anything," Abigail muttered. Sophie had shielded Harry as she had her daughters. He knew nothing. Sophie protected those she'd loved from certain danger.

"Tell me, what's going on?" he insisted.

"I don't know. Not yet. I'll be in touch as soon as I can. It's not safe now. Don't tell anyone you spoke to me. Don't try and call me. Delete all records of this call."

God, she sounded just like Stick did last time they'd spoken on the phone.

IT TOOK A FEW moments to compose herself, but she managed. She had to. For Stick and for Becky, so their lives wouldn't be lost in vain, like all the wasted lives at No Life and every other nightmare hellhole she'd endured. After a few deep breaths, she sat down and stared at the evidence before her. Many years ago, back at the Glasgow library where she'd hidden from life,

Abigail had taken a "Visual Illusions" book—and spent a day staring at the shapes on the pages until the face or the shape or the light-change jumped out at her. She used the same skill here, staring at the information on the flip charts . . .

At the letter from her mother.

At the table about the sample group in Granoch.

At the PA23 drink, at Joe's face, at the MMR shot he received much too late in life.

At the Graffiti Tease paintings.

At her iPhone.

At The Book of Remembrance.

She thought about everything that had happened since she came to LA: Becky, Stick, Grahame, Melanie. *Joe.* She stared. She detached herself, as Joe had been detached. She focused.

Then, quite suddenly, the pieces came together. The shape she'd waited for had formed. It was obvious and clear, as clear as the sunlight pouring through the Winnebago windows.

IN ONLY A FEW minutes, Abigail had assumed head cop in this investigation. Even Bren's father seemed okay with it. She stood before the McDowell family, pointing to the flip charts.

"Okay, so this is what I think: my father and Stick's father are part of Granoch. They tested PA23 on young people in Scotland in 1996. My mum knew and disapproved. It was illegal, so they had to shut her up. They must have threatened to hurt her, and me and Becky, and made up the paranoid schizophrenia story. They waited years to be sure the drug worked. The sample group turned out to be law-abiding and conformist adults, just as they hoped. Seventeen years later, they decided to roll it out in the United States. Stick and Becky cottoned on. They were going to tell the world, to stop it. Graffiti Tease was their way of doing it . . ."

Abigail's voice caught. *Idiot kids,* she thought. *Stupid, beautiful, spoiled, misguided idiot kids. No idea about how cold and ugly the world really is.*

She grabbed a barbeque fork from the tiny Winnebago sink and waved it at the papers stuck to the wall. "But Granoch found out about what they were up to. Grahame was monitoring her. They killed Becky so she wouldn't interfere. They already had a plan to give it out to the Juvies. They disguised it with an MMR shot. One of the Graffiti Tease kids, a good friend of Becky's, Joe Dixon, was one of the first to have it. He was behind the art, behind the whole campaign. He was a *genius* with his graffiti. And I saw him after. He was like a zombie. All that talent and drive, it was gone."

She paused and put the barbecue fork down. "That's all I know." She took the breath she desperately needed, paused, and looked at Bren. His mouth was half open. Grace was sickly white. Craig's temple was twitching.

"Does it make sense?" she asked, as much of herself as of Bren's family. "I mean, does it make sense Grahame would kill his own child? Who would *do* that?"

"Somebody who doesn't love their own child," Bren answered.

"My God," his mother and father whispered at the same time.

"So what are we going to do?" Bren asked.

Abigail lifted the Book of Remembrance and turned to the

page where she'd glued the deathbed letter her mother had written at the Western Infirmary. She touched the signature at the bottom, which she thought her mother had misspelled. Moving her finger gently over the two words, she whispered, "*Stophie Them.*" It was only when she spoke the words out loud that she allowed herself to accept their message.

She looked up, no longer afraid or angry, but fiercely determined.

"We're going to do what my mother wanted all along."

ABIGAIL COULDN'T HAVE ASKED for better allies than Gracie and Craig. She decided that she wouldn't think about her misinterpretation of Bren and what he thought that their relationship might be or could be. Bren wanted to protect her; that was all that mattered. Craig eventually even convinced her that calling the police was a bad idea. If Grahame had connections in Immigration at LAX, he might have connections with the LAPD, too.

Craig dialed an old university pal at Interpol whom he trusted implicitly. Within minutes, they had traced the number plate of the black car that had chased Abigail and Stick: 4DMSP38. As suspected, it turned out to be a company car, registered to GJ Prebiotics. Abigail waited for Craig to add any word of Stick—news of seventeen-year-old Matthew Howard being pulled from the Venice canals, dead or alive. But there was no word, not among the news or the authorities. Craig hung up the phone with a sigh.

"We have to find a way to stop Granoch," Abigail said.

"How are we going to do that?" Bren asked in a dry voice. "You do realize that you might as well have said, 'We should establish world peace.'"

She couldn't tell if Bren were more frightened than the rest of them, or just annoyed that Abigail's priority was Stick. But it didn't matter. The last thing she wanted to do was put another friend in danger. And that's what Bren was above all else: a friend.

"Maybe we should drop you somewhere safe," Gracie suggested, as if reading Abigail's mind. "Like Uncle Jamie's."

"Why, you don't think I'm tough enough?" Bren demanded.

"Of course not," Craig said. "But this is dangerous."

"I *know*." Bren crossed his arms in front of him.

Abigail felt a twinge of guilt. She'd incorrectly assumed he was gay; now she assumed he'd be scared.

"First things first," she said. "Let's find out what happened to Stick."

It was a two-hour drive back to Los Angeles. They were low on gasoline, so Craig stopped at the first service station en route.

"You need anything?" Bren asked.

She shook her head.

When the others left the Winnebago, Abigail picked up Becky's iPhone, keyed in the pin, and opened the video montage. Her sister's face filled the screen. Becky was wearing the same plain white T-shirt Abigail was wearing now. As much as it pained Abigail to watch, a weight had been lifted. Becky hadn't killed herself. She hadn't orchestrated the fast-forward bonding day because she knew it was going to be her last. She simply wanted Abigail to become a part of her life as quickly as possible. Abigail wasn't to blame. Of course, the truth was far darker than that initial suspicion. Becky had been murdered— either by Grahame or by his colleagues.

Abigail switched off the phone and shoved it in her pocket. She glanced out the window. Bren's parents were standing in line at the counter. Gracie wrapped her arm around her husband's shoulder. The gesture was thoughtless, familiar, and loving all at once. It occurred to Abigail that she'd never actually seen a committed couple in real life, a *lifelong* couple. Gracie and Craig didn't get along all the time; the dynamic was hardly perfect, but their devotion was solid and unspoken. It just *was*. As was their love for their son. The couples at the commune preached love, but that love was fragile and overdramatic, the devotion fleeting.

The door flew open.

"Bren, when did your parents meet?" Abigail asked.

It wasn't Bren. It was a man in a dark suit. Abigail tried to scream, but he clamped a cloth over her mouth and nose before she could move. An overpowering stench filled her nostrils, a combination at odds with itself: disinfectant and rotten garbage. Another man appeared behind him and darted for her legs. Her last thought as they dragged her from the Winnebago was *I'm either being killed or knocked unconscious*. Then there was only darkness.

CHAPTER SEVENTEEN

Abigail first noticed the pain in her arms. She couldn't move them. Everything else seemed like television interference. She tried to speak. *Is there someone there? Where am I?* Her mouth was dry, stretched, stuffed. If only she could make a sound. And the thirst. She needed water.

"Don't be scared." A wobbly figure appeared through the fuzz.

It was a man.

Her arms tensed. She tried to kick. She couldn't move her legs, either. Her limbs were bound. *Jesus Christ.* She was gagged and tied to a chair. Her underside ached. What had happened? What was her last clear memory? Two men had taken her. Suffocated her with a smelly cloth. She'd been kidnapped. And now a man was standing over her. Abigail tried to scream through the gag. A muted growl was all she managed. She bit at it, gnawed. There was no getting through the thick cotton material.

"I mean it, Abigail," the man continued.

Grahame. Of course. Who else?

"There really is nothing to worry about." The fuzziness cleared. He turned to someone across the room. "Go on, tell her . . ."

"There really is nothing to worry about," another voice confirmed.

Her heart pounded, filling her ears with a rapid *thump-thump-thump.* She looked to her right: nothing but a closed door. Ahead, past her father: a desk, with a small box on it. To the left: Dennis Howard, Stick's father, who nodded sadly. His eyes were bloodshot, his features drawn, haggard, and pained. She searched that terrible face for an answer and got it.

"I don't blame you for Matthew's death," he said and sniffed. "But I am heartbroken."

Liar! She wanted to scream. She moaned, tears on her cheeks, soaking the gag. So Stick was dead. She knew that for certain now. She also knew that he wasn't heartbroken that he'd lost his son; he was heartbroken that his son wasn't the perfect little boy he'd demanded him to be.

"We're both devastated," Grahame added. "But we are here to help you."

By now, everything had sharpened into stark focus: the dark wood, the desk, the filing cabinet, the locked door. This was her father's den. Her pulse raced even faster. What about Bren and his parents? Were they safe? Had Grahame and Dennis Howard killed them too?

"The family with the Winnebago, the McDowells . . . do you know where they live?" Stick's father asked. Grahame shot him an unreadable look, then turned back toward Abigail and kneeled in front of her, resting his hand on her shoulder.

"You know we'll find your friends eventually, Abigail," her father murmured. "In a few minutes I'll ask you where they might be. They're not at your friend Brendan's house. You'll tell me because you'll want to tell me. You'll tell because you'd know I'd never hurt you."

So they don't know where Bren and his parents are, she thought, blinking rapidly. *Somehow they must have escaped. Craig and Gracie are smart and have connections.*

"Abigail?" Grahame asked.

"Kill me, you shit—see if I care!" she shouted. But muffled in her gag it came out gibberish: "*Kmyoushseeffcrr!*" Her eyes blazed, defiant.

Grahame sighed. He walked over to the table, opened the box with the coded lock, and took out a pre-prepared syringe. *PA23.*

He moved toward her. The thudding in her ears drowned out every other sound. She fought desperately to move. Couldn't. Panic took over. She realized now that she'd prefer to die. Better dead than like Joe: a robot. Of all the ironies! Snapping into "robot mode" to avoid reality . . . now that the gift of an eternal robot mode was staring her in the face at the end of a moist needle, she knew what a bloody fool she'd been.

Her thoughts raced down a series of blind alleys, anything to escape. Becky had said something else about the den. No, not *said;* she'd texted. What? Floaty letters moved around before her eyes — *T h i n k*. She tried to imagine the page in her Book of Remembrance where she'd written it down. She tried to will the letters to form words. What was written in the text? Something about taffy and changing something . . . right?

But she couldn't quite remember or cling to the words. They'd read like nonsense.

Focus!

"I want to explain this to you, Abigail." Grahame sat on a chair beside her and touched her cheek. "The only thing this does is help you solve your problems. Look at Melanie. Life of hard knocks. She begged me for this after we got together. Now she's perfect." He tapped the end of the needle and dabbed Abigail's arm with an antiseptic wipe. "The whole mess could have been so easily avoided. But life gives us second chances. Becky's in the ground and Matthew's body is lost at the bottom of a canal. If they'd had this, they'd both be alive and happy. Sophie, too. But I have Melanie. I have you. And Dennis has his wife."

Abigail wriggled. Her shoulders tensed; her legs kicked at the ties. She could no longer think. She was a trapped animal.

"Becky was just like her mother," her father said. "So inquisitive and fiery. Oh, dear Becky. She got herself into so much trouble."

Abigail growled.

"But you should know, too, I had nothing to do with her death, or Matthew's. It wasn't right. We *are* furious. So many ideas in our group. Some people, well they're straying, taking a wrong path. It's not about hurting people. It's about making things better. We'll find a way to deal with what they did. But you have to believe me: I'll never let anyone harm you. You're my long-lost little girl. My only child now."

He pressed the needle against her skin. She struggled against the ties.

"Listen to your father," Mr. Howard said. "He's luckier than I am. He has a second chance. With Matthew gone, I have no future."

"This really is the best thing that could happen to you," Grahame said. "In less than a minute, you'll feel *relieved*. We can't just let kids kill themselves and each other and go nowhere, can we? You know that I'm right. Becky knew it, too. You agree with me. Your upbringing nearly destroyed you, and you long for peace. Now close your eyes for me." He paused and kissed her on the forehead. "I love you."

Abigail closed her eyes—not because he'd ordered her to, but because she was terrified.

She shuddered as her skin was pierced.

So this was it. Abigail Thom, once 50837, was about to disappear. She was as dead as Becky and Stick. Robust, closed-off, intelligent Abigail Thom—who loved Nieve, who hated Glasgow and the rain and social workers and children's homes and hostels and Billy and heroin and the monarchy, who wanted to go to University, who craved a new life and a family and adventures and opportunities, who mourned a sister called Becky and a boy called Stick, who was overwhelmed by the discovery that her mother wasn't a crazy bitch from hell but someone who loved her—LOVED her—and was also loved by some blond sculptor from the borders, and who had made three lifelong friends called Bren, Gracie, and Craig . . .

That Abigail Thom was about to disappear.

Grahame withdrew the needle and dabbed her arm again. He quickly covered the injection site with a Band-Aid. She counted back from sixty in horror. It would only take a minute, he said. 59. 58. 57. 56. 55. 54. 53. 52. 51. 50. 49 . . . What was she supposed to feel again? 48. 47. 46 . . . 43 . . . *Happy. Calm.* She kept counting, on and on and on. Her raging heartbeat provided the rhythm, never slowing.

9. 8. 7. 6. 5. 4 . . .

Calm happy content glad numb right good perfect . . .

3.

2.

1.

Gone.

She opened her eyes and inhaled through her nose. Or tried. She was hyperventilating, but maybe that was because she'd held her breath. She didn't feel any of the above. She still wanted to kick and scream and howl. She didn't though, because she was frozen in fear, waiting to be extinguished.

Maybe she'd counted too fast.

She waited.

Was the hot anger in her chest diminishing? The fury? The sadness?

No.

A few more minutes, perhaps.

She waited, the two men standing over her, watching.

But no, the rage and the pain only seemed to grow. She would kill these creepy screw-up excuses for men if she could. She would grab something sharp and heavy and smash them over their heads. She would kick, scream, hit, bite—*destroy*. It wasn't peace and calm that she felt. It was the exact opposite.

"You're feeling better, yes?" her father said. So she was right, it should have worked by now. "It's a warm feeling, isn't it? Everything just seems right."

The men stood back and studied her expression. She didn't move. She eyed them back, surreptitiously taking her surroundings. *The paperweight.* That'd smash a skull in. When they untied her, that's what she'd use. But why was she thinking such thoughts? Shouldn't those thoughts have been extinguished? She glanced at the lockbox, the one with the vials. The words from Becky's text came back to her, clear as if she were reading them fresh.

he has a box full of it in his den. i think he's going to do me. he thinks it'll help. i changed it. like the taffy.

Becky had changed it. The drug, she had changed the drug. *Like the taffy.* There was no PA23 in her bloodstream. *Saltwater . . .* like the taffy. The very last words her sister had spoken to her: the bowl of saltwater taffy that wasn't in her room. It was code. She'd known Abigail was in danger. And so she'd replaced the vials with saline, a placebo: a dose of nothingness. *Oh, Becky.* Oh beautiful, determined, vibrant, cool, inquisitive, wonderful, clever Becky. She'd saved her own sister, but couldn't save herself.

"Do you feel the warmth?" Her father smiled at her.

"Does everything feel good?" Mr. Howard smiled at her.

Abigail smiled back. She forced her breathing to an even in-and-out. She relaxed her shoulders. She deadened her eyes. And she nodded.

CHAPTER EIGHTEEN

For seven years, Abigail Thom had practiced being a robot. It was hard at first. Like when she'd made the mistake of getting close to that first social worker, Jason McVeigh. But after a while, it became automatic. *Don't let anyone in. Don't let anyone know what you're thinking, or how you're feeling. Do what you've got to do to survive.*

As they removed her gag, curious, Abigail steeled herself in "robot mode" and multiplied it by a million. She shape-shifted into the expressionless, past-less, personality-less zombie they wanted her to be. And above all, she told the truth. It was so much easier that way, especially now that she had nothing to hide. She told them all she knew about the McDowell family: that they might be at the hairdresser's or travelling around in the Winnebago. She told Grahame and Dennis these things because she knew Bren's family wouldn't be stupid enough to let themselves get caught.

"Good girl," her father said. "You're a good girl."

So she was. She would be—for as long as it took to escape.

That night, she sank into the bath Melanie poured for
her. She went to the bed Melanie made for her. And she said:
"Goodnight, Dad. Goodnight, Melanie."

"Why don't you call me Mom?" Melanie said, holding her
hand.

Abigail smiled. A robot wouldn't feel flesh crawling at the
touch of an alien lizard. A robot would feel nothing. "Goodnight, Mom."

AT 3:30 A.M.—CONFIDENT MELANIE and Grahame were
asleep—Abigail snuck downstairs to the den and turned on
the computer. Bren's hairdressing salon in LA came up in her
Google search, but there was surprisingly little online about
Brendan McDowell. She created a fake Facebook account,
searched until she found two people who might possibly be
matches, and composed a careful message.

> From: Stuffthemonarchy
> To: @brenmcdowell @graciemcdowell
> Message: Hey! Argyll is beautiful this time of year. Much
> healthier than LA.

She noticed there was next to nothing on both profiles: no
personal info, no photo, no posts. Either they rarely used Facebook, or they'd deleted everything. *Please let it be the latter.* She
pressed SEND, deleted the browsing history, and wiped the keyboard with a cloth. Then she crept back upstairs, and prayed.
Please let them get the message. Please let them get away.

THE FOLLOWING AFTERNOON, HER dad informed her that she would be going to boarding school in England, and quite soon. He'd decided it was probably the best idea to return to a more familiar environment. As if a posh London boarding school and the Glasgow streets were remotely similar, other than being part of the United Kingdom. Abigail smiled and nodded. She smiled and nodded at everything.

Later, she heard her dad on the phone in the den. "Well, keep looking!" he barked angrily. "People don't just disappear! This isn't just a loose end!"

She stifled a squeal of joy. Grahame hadn't found the McDowells yet.

Dennis Howard came for dinner that night. He sat at the table, pontificating with her father about the positive changes they'd noticed, encouraging her to chime in.

"People are already noticing the improved behavior in the country's Juvenile Halls," he said. "We've had to be discreet. But it'll be no time before we can bring our research out in the open. They'll vote for this! It will become as common as the Rubella vaccine. All that we've ever been missing is a control."

Melanie gazed at him through dull eyes. "A control?"

"We've never conducted a clinical test, where we've given a group of subjects a placebo. To prove PA23: to prove that the control group's behavior doesn't change, whereas those who have received the drug *do* change. And for the better."

What about me, you glorious idiots? Abigail felt like screaming.

"Don't you agree, Abigail?" Grahame prodded.

"Oh yes," she said.

"Oh yes," Melanie echoed.

"Dessert, anyone?" Grahame asked.

Abigail kept smiling and dabbed her lips with a napkin. *One day I'm going to plunge a knife into your twisted black heart.* "Dessert sounds lovely," she said.

OVER THE NEXT SEVEN days she pretended to like poached eggs. She listened to Melanie go on and on and on about how to tackle the redecoration of the dining room. She nodded as her father wrote off Becky as an "inevitable sacrifice for a greater cause."

For seven days, she snuck down to her father's den in the middle of the night to check if there were any messages for stuffthemonarchy (none); she smiled and nodded; she sat in the sun and kicked her feet in the pool, alone with Melanie.

For seven days, she went mad.

But tomorrow it would all be over. Tomorrow, she was off to boarding school. Not just any boarding school: Rodean. The very boarding school Becky couldn't hack.

After breakfast, Melanie asked Abigail to collect the mail.

"Sure, Mom," Abigail said.

As she removed the pile of letters from the mailbox, her heart jumped. The top letter was addressed to her. She quickly slipped it down her jeans and walked back inside.

"I'm going up to finish packing," she called to the kitchen. She placed the letters on the kitchen bench, fighting every impulse to run up the stairs. *A robot doesn't run.* She walked slowly instead, shut the bedroom door, shut the bathroom door—and, once she was sitting on the toilet with the overhead fan at full blast—she opened the envelope as quietly as she could.

> *Dearest Abigail,*
>
> *You are a difficult person to find! God willing this letter reaches you. I am writing to say thank you from the bottom of my heart. Your money enabled me to bring my family to Edinburgh. My mum is on a dialysis machine now and is coping much better. I am studying for beauty school! Because of you my mother is alive and I am happy.*
>
> *I would love to see you. If you are ever in Edinburgh, please come and stay with us. My address is 78 Kitchler Street, Edinburgh and my telephone number is 0131 555 9835.*
>
> > *With love and with eternal gratitude,*
> > *Camelia*

ABIGAIL CHECKED OVER THE contents of her new Louis Vuitton suitcase. Three sets of school uniforms, twelve sets of matching underwear, twenty pairs of socks, ten pairs of tights, school shoes, sports gear, swimsuit, four pairs of pajamas, one dressing gown, and seven after-school/weekend outfits (three skirts, three blouses, one pair of trousers, one pair of flat shoes). And, yes, a raincoat. She was about to close it when she remembered something.

She reached under the bed, grabbed the three library books she'd brought with her from Glasgow, and tucked them under the raincoat.

"You ready?" Grahame yelled from the hall.

"Ready!" she said zipping the case.

THE GREY AUDI CONVERTIBLE dropped her at the front of International Departures. The airport was familiar to her this time. She didn't feel scared or nervous at all. And now she even had her own passport: real name and all, fresh post-injection smiling photo taken just in time.

"Goodbye, Dad," she said, hugging him.

"Use this to phone me," he said, handing her a mobile phone.

"Thanks, I will."

"Goodbye, Mom."

Two kisses, a hug. "Don't be a stranger!" Melanie said cheerily.

Abigail waved and smiled as they drove off. When they were out of sight, she let out a burst of air. It was as if she'd been holding her breath ever since she'd woken up bound and gagged in the chair in Grahame's den.

"Good riddance!" she shouted, just as she had when she'd left Glasgow all those weeks ago. "Good fucking riddance, you bastards!"

SCOTLAND IS NOT ENGLAND, Abigail thought as she stared out the train window. England was like the kids who'd had the shot: tame, neat, and well-managed. Scotland was like the toe-rags who hadn't. England was a blur outside the window, fading rapidly. Quaint cottages. Organized fields. Rolling hills. Pretty sheep. Peace. Calm.

She texted her father as the train plowed northward. *Arrived safely.*

He texted her back seconds later: *That's good. Want to hear about your dorm and roommate once you're settled in.*

Of course he did. If her roommate was trouble, he'd be on the first plane over to deliver a shot of PA23. Too bad that would never happen.

Attending Rodean would have been a privilege and an honor for most kids. Not Abigail. There was a Nobel Laureate on staff, not to mention countless other revered academics, all of whom intimidated the new arrivals. Not Abigail. An imposing cluster of white buildings perched on the cliffs south of London—with gorgeous landscaped gardens that overlooked the sea, an indoor pool . . . any person, new student or not, would gasp in awe at Rodean. Not Abigail. No, because in a matter of hours, Abigail wouldn't even be in England anymore.

CAMELIA LAST TRIED TO hug Abigail in the Glasgow airport. Abigail had fled that embrace. Here, at the door of the small mews house in Edinburgh, she practically leapt into Camelia's arms.

"It's so good to see you," Abigail whispered, holding her tight. "You have no idea."

Once Camelia had accepted what Abigail had told her, most of it an exhausted jumble, Camelia agreed to share a taxi with her to Argyll. It was pouring with rain when they arrived. Wet, wet Scotland. But after weeks of nonstop sunshine, Abigail drank it in. She lifted her face up to the sky, felt the drops tickle her face, and rubbed the water into her skin.

She gazed at the still grey mass that was Holy Loch. Her mother's ashes were in there somewhere.

"Hi, Mum," she whispered. "I made it out. I'm free."

She had no idea if Bren and his parents remembered that this is where she came from, or if they got the Facebook message, or if they even understood it. It was a desperate hope, but that's all she could cling to. That, and Camelia's hand—which she kept gripping, knuckles white, as they walked toward the commune. The ramshackle encampment was just as she remembered it: filthy, colorful vans and filthy, colorful people. Several adults were cooking sausages on the barbecue in spite of the rain, huddled under a makeshift tent. Vegetarian, no doubt. A group of kids were squealing, playing Rounders on the shore of the loch. She didn't recognize a single one of them.

Her heart sank. What was she expecting? How would they ever find their way here? And what would she do now? Hide out in Edinburgh, as Camelia kept insisting? For how long? And then what? She stopped at the edge of the settlement, faint. The last time she'd had a decent night's sleep was far in the past. She'd been faking for too long.

Camelia must have noticed. "Hey, stop. Look at me. We'll find them, maybe not here, but we will. I'm going to help you. Okay?"

"Okay." She wiped the warm rain from her eyes and looked

at her friend. Then she noticed something over Camelia's shoulder: A large white trailer tucked amongst lush green trees, about a hundred feet from the edge of the settlement. Her heart leapt.

"What is it?"

"The stickers . . ." The trailer was plastered with them. NO NUKES! STOP GLOBAL WARMING! VOTE FOR INDEPENDENCE! But it was the last that caught her eye: STUFF THE MONARCHY! Abigail ran and grabbed at the door handle, not even thinking about knocking.

It was locked. She heard people moving inside, then a tentative female voice. "Who's that?"

Abigail ventured: "Stuff the monarchy?"

The door opened an inch and an eye peered through the crack. Before she could work out whose eye it was, the door opened fully. *Gracie.* Dressed in jeans and a Scottish National Party T-shirt, Bren's mum threw her arms around Abigail.

"You made it. Oh, you're here! Are you okay?" She moved back to look at her, smiling, then noticed Camelia. "Who's this?"

"My friend Camelia. Don't worry, she's one of us."

"Quick, inside."

The van looked just like the Winnebago in California: a Police Operations Room complete with flip charts, maps, photos, computers, printers. The door to the bedroom area was closed. Craig smiled tiredly from the table. Abigail smiled back, her eyes welling with tears. It wasn't the caravan she grew up in, but the feeling inside was the same. It wasn't Nieve who waited for her, but that feeling was the same, too. Abigail belonged here. For whatever twisted reason, this was home. She'd come home.

"Bren?" she asked nervously.

"Laying low with his uncle in Las Vegas," Gracie said. "He thought we might need someone on the ground over there. When the time's right, we'll contact him."

"We're going to need all the help we can get," Craig said.

She nodded. *Two deaths so far*, Abigail thought. *And hundreds, maybe thousands, of brain deaths.* They were going to need an army. She looked at Gracie, Craig, and Camelia. "For now it's just us." She wasn't being defeatist, but she *was* terrified. Now that she'd found the McDowells and knew they were safe, a whole new set of realities set in. "Us four."

"Five! Just give me a second."

It took her a moment to realize the voice had come from behind the door.

That voice! Her heart thudded, that all-encompassing *thump-thump-thump* she'd felt in the chair. Only this time, it wasn't horror or panic. She looked at Gracie and then at Craig. They both nodded toward the door. She walked toward it slowly, as if in a dream. Her ankles felt like jelly. It couldn't be. Could it be? She was too scared to open it and see, in case she was wrong. She stood before it, held her hand out . . .

He opened it before she could. "Thank God you made it, Abi," Stick said.

The bulge from a thick bandage protruded from under his plain white T-shirt. His face was deathly white. He must have lost ten pounds; his eyes were hollow and sunken. He looked like a Glasgow street urchin. But that didn't stop her from hurling herself at him.

"They found me," he murmured, squeezing her back.

Abigail opened her eyes and turned to Gracie, who nodded, but whose face had also turned pale; she seemed to shudder at the memory. "He crawled out of the water and back to Bren's place. He passed out in a closet, trying to hide. There was a lot of blood."

"I would have died if the McDowells hadn't found me."

"We pumped him full of intravenous fluid and monitored him day and night on the run for seventy-two hours," Gracie explained, her Scottish accent suddenly thickening.

Abigail placed her hands on Stick's face. She wasn't imagining it, he was real. Without thinking twice, she kissed him. For a moment, everything but his lips disappeared. But only for a moment, because when she opened her eyes she noticed the Book of Remembrance she'd made for Becky. She took Stick's hand, moved toward the table, and touched the book gently.

"Granoch is more powerful, wealthy, and dangerous than I could have imagined," Craig commented, as if reading her mind. "I didn't want to buy it at first. But they cover their tracks in a way I've never seen before. Not to mention that they kill their own children."

The last words sent a fresh wave of pain through Abigail. With it came rage. *Those bastards.* She girded her strength, not robot strength, but real strength. "That's true," she replied. "But Grahame said something to me right before he gave me the shot, right before I knew Becky had saved me. The Granoch group fights amongst themselves. There's a split among them between what's acceptable and what isn't. My father and Stick's father were on the same side. I really do believe that they didn't want Becky or Stick to die. The others don't care as much."

Gracie stepped toward her. "So what are you saying?"

"I'm saying that at least we're united. We're one, and they aren't. That's strength."

"We are one," Stick echoed, squeezing her hand.

Abigail nodded. "And we have lots of work to do."

ACKNOWLEDGMENTS

HUGE thanks to my editor at Soho Teen, Daniel Ehrenhaft, who nurtured this from its conception, offering the perfect mix of excitement, encouragement, and knuckle-wrapping. Thanks to my agent at Jenny Brown Associates, Lucy Juckes, for loving this project and guiding me through each draft. A big mushy ta to my husband, Sergio, for brainstorming, researching, reading drafts, and generally being ace. And to my raw material—my children—Anna and Joe, who have never read any of my books but quite like the sound of this one.